A Pass

By the same author

Freedman
Soldier, Sail North
The Wheel of Fortune
Last in Convoy
The Mystery of the *Gregory Kotovsky*
Contact Mr Delgado
Across the Narrow Seas
Wild Justice
On Desperate Seas
The Liberators
The Angry Island
The Last Stronghold
The Golden Reef
Find the Diamonds
The Plague Makers
Whispering Death
Three Hundred Grand
Crusader's Cross
A Real Killing
Special Delivery
The Spanish Hawk
Ten Million Dollar Cinch
The Deadly Shore
The Rodriguez Affair
The Murmansk Assignment
The Sinister Stars
Sea Fury
Watching Brief
Weed
Away With Murder
Ocean Prize
A Fortune in the Sky
Search Warrant
The Marakano Formula
Cordley's Castle
The Haunted Sea
The Petronov Plan
Feast of the Scorpion
The Honeymoon Caper
A Walking Shadow
The No-Risk Operation
Final Run
Blind Date
Something of Value
Red Exit
The Courier Job
The Rashevski Icon
The Levantine Trade
The Spayde Conspiracy
Busman's Holiday
The Antwerp Appointment
Stride
The Seven Sleepers
Lethal Orders
The Kavulu Lion
A Fatal Errand
The Stalking-Horse
Flight to the Sea
A Car for Mr Bradley
Precious Cargo
The Saigon Merchant
Life-Preserver
Dead of Winter
Come Home, Toby Brown
Homecoming
The Syrian Client
Poisoned Chalice
Where the Money Is
A Dream of Madness
Paradise in the Sun
Dangerous Enchantment
The Junk Run
Legatee
Killer
Dishonour Among Thieves
Operation Zenith
Dead Men Rise Up Never
The Spoilers
With Menaces
Devil Under the Skin
The Animal Gang
Steel
The Emperor Stone
Fat Man from Colombia
Bavarian Sunset
The Telephone Murders
Lady from Argentina
The Poison Traders
Squeaky Clean
Avenger of Blood
A Wind on the Heath
One-Way Ticket
The Time of Your Life
Death of a Go-Between
Some Job
The Wild One
Skeleton Island

A Passage of Arms

JAMES PATTINSON

ROBERT HALE · LONDON

First published in Great Britain 2000

ISBN 0 7090 6617 1

Robert Hale Limited
Clerkenwell House
Clerkenwell Green
London EC1R 0HT

2 4 6 8 10 9 7 5 3 1

Typeset by
Derek Doyle & Associates, Liverpool.
Printed in Great Britain by
St Edmundsbury Press, Bury St Edmunds, Suffolk.
Bound by WBC Book Manufacturers Limited, Bridgend.

Contents

1

Super Tramp

The name of the ship lying alongside a wharf in the Russian port of Vladivostok was *W. H. Davies*. She was registered in Liberia, her home port being given as Monrovia; but she was owned by an Englishman who was also her captain. She had not always had her present name; indeed, it was the fourth she had had, passing in the course of more than three decades of life from one owner to another and taking on a different identity with each change of ownership.

The name was something of a private joke on the part of Daniel Gregg, the owner; for had not W. H. Davies, the Welsh poet, written *The Autobiography of a Super Tramp?* And was that not what this ship was – a tramp? Well, perhaps not super, not after all these years of wandering across the oceans of the world, but certainly a tramp, one of a breed that had not completely given way to the container ship and the freighter plane.

The *W. H. Davies* was a motor vessel of some four thousand tons net register, and had been built in a Tyneside shipyard which had long since shut up shop in the face of cutthroat competition from shipbuilders of the Far East. When new she had sailed under the Red Ensign; now, for convenience, as the expression was, she flew the flag of a West African republic and was registered in a port to which she never sailed. This was a cause of some regret to Captain Gregg; he would have preferred the old Red Duster to this red and white striped thing with a lone star in one corner. But it all came down to a question of finance and the avoidance of hampering regulations and trade union hassle.

Before becoming owner of the MV *W. H. Davies* Gregg had served for a number of years in the merchant navy, rising steadily in rank from apprentice to chief officer on board a bulk carrier. It was not what he would have chosen. By his reckoning there was no romance in it. Of course one could never go back to the days of sail when seafaring was an adventure and ships had a beauty that was lost forever in the leviathons of today; but surely there ought, he felt, to be something preferable to this.

So when the chance came to make a move he took it without a second thought. And he had never regretted the decision.

It came in the shape of a legacy: an aunt died and left her favourite nephew practically all she had. It was not a great fortune, but it was enough to put Gregg on a different tack. He left the bulk carrier and started looking around for something more to his taste. After a few months of searching he found what he wanted. It was not beyond his means as they were now constituted, and he bought it without a moment's hesitation.

The *Centaur* had at that stage in her career been owned by a small shipping company which operated mainly on the Baltic run with a variety of cargoes. This company had decided to upgrade its fleet and *Centaur* was one of those vessels due to be axed. She came up for sale and, not surprisingly, there was no immediate rush of buyers eager to gain possession of such an elderly ship. In fact Gregg appeared to be unique in that respect, and he was able to get her, if not just for a song, at least for considerably less than the whole opera.

In the event a complete refit cost more than the ship herself, but he regarded this as money well spent and did not begrudge it. It was his intention that the *W. H. Davies* should have many more years of service ahead of her, and in making a start under this new name she needed to be in as good a condition as was possible in the circumstances.

Gregg himself was no youngster at the time. He was thirty-five years old and had been married and divorced. He was still on amicable terms with his ex-wife and there had been no acrimony in the parting. They exchanged cards at Christmas and remembered each other's birthday, though not the anniversary of their wedding. She was married again, to a man named George Geary, a dry stick if ever there was one in Gregg's opinion. He could never understand what she saw in the man. But he was there; he had a job in the City and Patricia could rely on him to come home every day after work. He, Gregg, had been absent from the nest far more than he was in it, and perhaps she preferred someone who was always around; someone to keep her company and take her out for the evening now and then. Who could blame her?

Gregg was a rugged character, a shade under six feet in height, bony and muscular with hair like tow. The bosun of a ship he was in once told him that he was regarded by the crew as a tough cookie; and perhaps he was, though he had never thought of himself in that way. Perhaps, too, it was no bad thing for a ship's officer to have that kind of reputation. There could be some real tough cookies among the seamen who came under his command.

With the ship after her refit he could find little fault. No amount of refurbishment could make her the equal of a vessel fresh from the builder's yard, but for her age she was not bad, not bad at all. She would do.

He had by this time a partner in the business. Frank Loder was a somewhat younger man, and the two of them had become friends while serving together on board a freighter doing the Australian run. They had kept in touch since then, and Loder had been the first person Gregg had confided in regarding his decision to become a ship-owner. Loder thought it a great idea, and he was so enthusiastic that he suggested putting his own savings into the venture. Gregg had not hesitated to accept the offer, and it was thus that Loder had become junior partner in the shipping firm of Gregg and Loder, which boasted a house flag green in colour with the logo GL in the middle of it. A natural consequence of this move was that when the *W. H. Davies* eventually put to sea under the captaincy of Daniel Gregg, the mate was Frank Loder.

Loder was smaller than Gregg; some five feet eight inches in height and turning the scale at around ten and a half stone. It was unlikely that anyone had ever called him a tough cookie; his features were of the cherubic kind, his manner engaging, his voice devoid of any harshness. Yet if anyone had felt inclined to rate him as a pushover they would have been making a mistake. He could look after himself in any situation, as Gregg knew well from experience.

It happened late one evening in Sydney as they were making their way back to their ship. Two thugs jumped them in an alleyway and attempted a mugging. They were armed with knives, but they got more than they had bargained for. In a matter of seconds Loder had thrown his man to the ground and had taken away his knife. Gregg was having rather more trouble with his assailant but had avoided a knife thrust and had grappled with him. It was a pretty even struggle until Loder joined in; after that it was no contest. The entire engagement lasted no more than a couple of minutes before the would-be muggers were in full flight, leaving their knives behind them.

Gregg was amazed at the way Loder had performed, and said so.

Loder played it down. 'Judo. Nothing to it if you know the right way.'

'So where did you learn judo?'

Loder grinned. 'In Japan. Where else? I was serving on board a ship that was held up in Yokohama for repairs. Had time on my hands and took a course in the art from the masters. Thought it might come in handy sometime.'

'And it certainly has. You'll have to give me some lessons in the game.'

'Be glad to. Any time.'

The second and third mates were very young. One of them, Harry Park, the third mate, was just out of his apprenticeship. The other, Paul Langton, had made only a few voyages before joining the *W. H. Davies*. He was a bit of a roly-poly, podgy-faced and inclined to indolence, but a capable officer in spite of his lack of experience. Park was black-haired, rather tall and awkward, eager to please but nervously fearful of not measuring up to the responsibility which was now his. In him there was some of that romantic feeling for the seafaring life that possessed both Gregg and Loder. It was the career he had chosen of his own free will, while for his part Langton had rather drifted into it because he could think of nothing else that attracted him and an old sea dog of an uncle had told him that there was no finer calling for a lad of spirit. He was not sure he fitted that description, but the sea dog obviously believed he did and he was reluctant to disillusion the old boy. So he had allowed himself to be persuaded. He had to do something.

The chief engineer was an ancient compared with the deck officers. His name was Grimley and his head was as bald as a cannon ball. He was paunchy and waddled like a duck, and he seemed to have a permanent grievance with life, as though convinced that it had given him a raw deal. He spoke in a kind of whine and had a way of tugging at the lobe of his left ear, which, no doubt as the result of this treatment, had become noticeably longer than the other one.

Gregg did not care much for the look of Arthur Grimley at first sight, and longer acquaintance with the man did little to alter that original impression. But Grimley happened to be available at the crucial moment and no one else was, so in spite of a few qualms he took him on. The engineeer had the credentials to prove his competence, and that was really what mattered; an unprepossessing physical appearance was neither here nor there.

What he did not know, since the man himself had not felt obliged to reveal the fact, was that Grimley had served a term in jail. The offence for which he was locked away in one of Her Majesty's prisons was an assault on another of the Queen's subjects, causing him grievous bodily harm – GBH, as it was termed in the trade. To Grimley's way of thinking this was a most unjust punishment, bearing in mind the extent of the provocation. When a man returns home after a long sea voyage, however unexpected the arrival, he is surely entitled to feel somewhat aggrieved on finding another man in bed with his wife, especially when the other man happens to be an old friend.

Not that he had any great love for Vera. She was a bitch, that was the truth of it; but this was beside the point, and Joe Sims had no business crawling into bed with her when he was away. So he had surely had good reason for doing what he had done. A man had a right to protect his own, didn't he?

But the administrators of the law had not seen it in that light, possibly because in the course of upholding this undoubted right he had broken the intruder's jaw and inflicted sundry other injuries of varying severity, besides giving a few back-handers to his ever-loving wife when he had finished with her Lothario.

Nevertheless, Grimley regarded it as a shocking piece of injustice that he should have been deprived of his liberty simply for doing what any man in a similar situation might have been expected to do. He served his term with resignation because there was no alternative, but he resented the necessity and turned over in his mind ways and means by which he could make Joe and Vera pay for what they had done to him when he regained his freedom. He had still not worked out a way of doing this without repercussions for himself when the job as chief engineer of the *W. H. Davies* came up. And as he had to make a living he took it and postponed the settlement of that old score for a later time. It would keep.

The second engineer was a very different type of person. He was tall and thin and so self-effacing that it seemed probable that if he could have made himself invisible he would surely have done so. His name was Clegg, and the most notable feature about him was the size of his hands and feet. They were out of all proportion to the rest of his body, a fact of which he seemed to be only too painfully aware. He spoke little, and when he did it was in a voice that was scarcely more than a whisper. It was obvious that he stood in awe of his superior, and even feared him perhaps. Grimley was aware of the fact and took advantage of it to browbeat the other man. He was by nature a bully and possibly regarded Clegg as a stand-in for Joe Sims, who would eventually get what was coming to him but for the present could not be reached.

The bosun was a grizzled veteran named Walter Crane, a tough, heavy man with a long experience of the sea who had served in a great variety of ships. He knew his job and went about it with a minimum of fuss; but as to the rest of the deck crew, they were in his opinion a pretty poor lot. He had known better, but you had to make do with the material that came to hand and there was no sense in complaining, so he kept his thoughts to himself.

He was anyway approaching the time when his seagoing would come to an end; a few more years and he would swallow the anchor, as the saying was, and step ashore for good. What he would do with himself then he simply did not know. He had long lost touch with any other members of the family and he had no desire to look them up. His wife had left him years ago, so he would be on his own. Not much to look forward to. Maybe he ought to take a trip on board one of those monster pleasure liners that were nothing more nor less than floating holiday camps. The idea brought a twisted smile to his lips. Perish the thought!

*

Several months had elapsed between the time when Daniel Gregg and Frank Loder went into partnership in buying their ship and the day when she sailed on her maiden voyage under the new house flag. Gregg had a feeling that there should have been some kind of ceremony to mark the occasion; a bottle of champagne cracked on her bows perhaps. But there was nothing. Yet for the two men themselves it was the start of an era.

And now, years later, the ship was in Vladivostok. But much had happened in the course of those years between, some good, some bad. The *W. H. Davies* had carried a variety of cargoes to and from many different ports scattered around the world; but never before had she taken on board the kind of merchandise that was destined to be lowered into her holds very soon now.

It was a type of cargo Gregg had never anticipated handling, and he had misgivings about it even now. But the die was cast. The woman, who was indeed young enough to be called a girl, had persuaded him, doubtful as he had been. Loder had had doubts too, but he had been won over as well. Margarita had charm and could be very persuasive when she set her mind to it.

'She could make a man do anything,' Loder said. 'However crazy it might be.'

Gregg had smiled. 'So you feel that too?'

'Who wouldn't? If you ask me, she's got some devil in her.'

'I'm not asking you, Frankie. But you could be right. And it makes no difference.'

'I know, I know.'

It was cold in Vladivostok, though it was a long way from winter yet. The sky was like lead and a light fall of snow was giving the ships in harbour a ghostly look. Gregg shivered. It was the first time he had come to this port on the eastern extremity of the Russian Federation, and he was not favourably impressed. He hoped it might be his last visit. But who could foretell what the future might hold in store?

Not he. Not Captain Daniel Gregg of the MV *W. H. Davies*. That was for sure.

2

Hell of a Way to Go

For a time after getting the *W. H. Davies* into action they stuck to the short-haul trade across the North Sea, venturing no further than the Baltic. There were cargoes to be had and it suited the crew, since none of them was very long away from home. Things were shaking down very nicely, it seemed to Gregg, and he liked the feel of the ship; he could not have asked for anything better; certainly not at a price he could have paid. And she was his, his and Loder's; that was what made all the difference; that was the icing on the cake.

She was good in rough weather too. The North Sea in a winter gale could be hellish, but the old *W. H. Davies* took it in her stride. Standing in the wheelhouse and looking down upon the foredeck, Gregg would feel a thrill of pride as the bows nosed into the waves and came up dripping, while flecks of pale foam were whipped away by the wind. Ah, this was the life for him.

They went as far east as Finland and Estonia, as far north as Iceland, carrying mixed cargoes: machinery, manufactured goods, timber, paint, textiles, glassware, grain, anything that might be traded between one country and another. Sometimes it seemed to him that they were transporting certain goods in one direction and bringing back identical stuff on the return voyage; as if countries traded with one another just for the sake of trading.

But there was no easy money to be had; there was too much competition. It was a cut-throat business, and the container ships and the bulk carriers had taken the lion's share of it. Nevertheless, there was still something left for the minnows like the *W.H. Davies*, though you had to fight to get it.

They eventually broke away from the North Sea trade with a voyage to South Africa. They discharged the cargo in Cape Town under the shadow of Table Mountain and picked up another destined for Singapore.

And it was in Singapore that the trouble started.

It started when Walter Crane, the bosun, went ashore and did not return.

Gregg was not worried at first. The man had probably got stinking drunk in some dive and was sleeping it off. But on the second day of Crane's absence he decided to go to the police.

There was a station not far from where the ship was docked, and a young sergeant who appeared to be Chinese but spoke good English, listened politely to what he had to say, took down particulars and promised to attend to the matter. But in spite of the politeness Gregg had the impression that this was the kind of story the man had heard only too frequently. He doubted whether anything would really be done about it. It would be entered in the file and very soon forgotten. Or was that being too cynical? Perhaps they would do their very best to find the bosun. And perhaps it would be none too easy.

*

He was right about that. He was also on the mark in thinking that the bosun had been drinking fairly heavily in a rather seedy bar, frequented by a rough-looking sort of clientèle. Many of the customers had the appearance of being seamen; others were the kind of characters who habitually associated themselves with men from ships, who might have money in their pockets and might without too much difficulty be relieved of some, if not all, of it.

Crane had drawn an advance of pay and had a wad of the local currency. He hauled it out and peeled a note off the top to pay for his drink. In a dive like that it was a mistake that a man of his experience should have avoided. But he had already drunk enough to make him careless.

Suddenly he discovered a thin, black-haired, yellow-skinned man standing at his side by the bar. He was wearing black cotton trousers and a dirty white T-shirt and he started speaking with his mouth close to Crane's ear in a voice low enough in the general hubbub not to be heard by anyone else in the place. With those lips no more than a couple of inches from his right ear, Crane could hear quite clearly what the man was saying. Moreover, the fact that he did not elbow this importunate character aside or advise him in no uncertain terms to get to hell out of it indicated that whatever it was that was being breathed into that right ear was of more than a little interest to the bosun. And indeed, after a few minutes of low-toned conversation Crane drained his glass and left the smoky, alcohol-polluted atmosphere of the bar in company with the man in the dirty T-shirt.

It was late in the evening now, but the street outside was still bustling with humanity, and to Crane the air felt scarcely any cooler than it had been all day.

'Is it far?' he asked.

'No,' the man said. 'Not far. You come, you see. Pretty girl. You like pretty girl. Sure thing.'

'Yes, but how much is it going to cost?' Crane said. He was beginning to have doubts regarding the wisdom of allowing himself to be seduced by the picture of infinite delight painted for him by this dubious-looking stranger. Even in his rather fuddled state he was not devoid of all caution. 'What's it going to cost me?'

The man gave no direct answer. He grasped Crane's left arm just above the elbow and steered him down a side-street.

'This way, this way. Nearly there now.'

Crane put up no resistance but allowed himself to be urged along, only hazily aware of his surroundings, the traffic on the street, the throng of people on foot brushing past, the mingled sounds, human and mechanical, like a kind of buzzing in his ears, and the man tugging at his arm.

'Not far now, sailor. Soon be there.'

It was in a narrow lane. The doorway was open. They went up a flight of bare wooden stairs and along a corridor that was almost in darkness. The man pushed open a door and a moment later Crane found himself in a hot stuffy little room, sparsely furnished with a bed, a couple of hard chairs and a dressing-table. The illumination was provided by one low-power electric bulb with no shade.

Even in his fuddled state Crane knew that he had been gulled. This was no palace of delights such as he had been led to expect, and it was no pretty young girl sitting on one of the chairs and treating him to a gap-toothed smile of greeting – a smile that was more of a leer than anything else; repellent rather than inviting.

The sight stopped him in his tracks and he heard the door close behind him. The woman rose from the chair and advanced a step. She was wearing a dirty cotton dress which hung on her skinny frame like a rag. Her feet were bare and grimy.

'No,' Crane said. 'Get away from me, you old hag.'

He turned, with the intention of leaving at once. He had been really taken in; he should have known better; he with his experience. It was the drink that had done it, the alcohol clouding his brain, ruining his judgement. But this was as far as it went; he had come to his senses and would be moving out, right now, no hanging around. Hell's bells! He should have known.

But when he turned he saw that the man in the dirty T-shirt was standing between him and the door, barring his way of retreat.

'Move over,' Crane said. 'Lemme pass, you yeller bastard.'

The man did not move. He said: 'You no go now. You come, you pay, you take nice girl. All fine.'

'What girl?' Crane demanded. 'I don't see no bloody girl. All I see's a soddin' pimp and an old hag what's run to seed long ago. You don't get me paying for that. Goods not as advertised, see? You could be had up on a charge of false pretences. That's against the law, that is. You could be put in the slammer for less.'

Whether any of this was getting through to the one on the receiving end was doubtful. But whether it was getting through or not, one thing was certain – it was having no effect on his determination to prevent Crane from leaving. He stood his ground, backed up against the door and not budging an inch. He even had the nerve to extend an open hand, palm upward. His voice came like a hiss.

'You pay now, sailor. Fifty dollars. Then I go. Leave you here. You have good time with girl. Fifty dollars. Low price.'

'Fifty dollars for that!' Crane jerked a thumb at the woman and spoke with contempt. 'You must be crazy – or reckon I am. Fifty Singapore dollars! That's around twenty-five quid in real money. And even if you offered to pay me that to have her I wouldn't take it. So get away from that door and I'll be going. Pronto.'

Still the man did not move. And when he spoke there was a note of threat in his voice.

'You pay now, sailor. Best for you if you pay now and take woman. She good. You bet.'

'Like hell, she is! Maybe was one day. Long ago. Past her prime now. Past her shelf life, that's for sure. Step aside, old man, step aside.'

But the man did not step aside. His voice came even more hissingly, the threat in it unmistakable.

'You make trouble, sailor? Not wise. Best you make no trouble. Best for you and best for me. You want trouble, you get it.'

Crane was well aware of the threat but did not give a damn. What could one leathery old guy and a scraggy woman do to him? They had no idea who they were dealing with. A man with his experience of handling tough ship's crews was no pushover even if he had taken on board a drop or two of liquor. He could still look after himself if it came to a bit of violence, as they would soon find out if they tried any fancy stuff.

'Trouble!' he said. 'You don't know what trouble is. So just don't start anything, see?'

That was when he felt the woman clawing at him. She had come up from behind and had flung her bony arms round his neck. He gave her an elbow in the guts and she let out a squawk and fell away from him. The man seemed to take offence at this treatment of the woman, and he took a swipe at Crane. It was more of a slap than a punch; it hit him on the cheek and it stung. This angered him, and in retaliation he launched a haymaker which knocked the pimp sideways, so that he almost lost his balance and staggered away from the door.

'Right,' Crane said. 'That's it. Now I'm going.'

He had his hand on the doorknob when the woman came at him again. She had got her breath back and was beating a tattoo on the back of his head with her fists. She was not hurting him much, but it was annoying, like the buzzing around of a persistent fly. He turned away from the man and caught her wrists and pushed her back towards the bed. The edge of it came into contact with the backs of her legs and she fell over backwards with Crane on top of her. Her face was close to his, and she spat at him. This was another annoyance, and he lost his temper and clouted her on the jaw with a fist like iron.

'Take that, you bitch!'

He might have added some more, but something whipped round his neck and tightened on his throat, cutting off his power of speech. It felt like wire or a thin cord, and it was biting into him and hurting like hell. He could not breathe, and he clawed at it with his fingers but could get no grip. He could feel a hard object pressing into the small of his back and he guessed that it was the man's knee. And it was this same man who was holding the cord or the wire and using the knee for leverage as he kept the ligature tight, the ligature that was remorselessly strangling him.

It came into Crane's mind that he had reached the end of the line. It was a hell of a way to go. And for what? For the sake of a few stinking Singapore dollars, which he could have handed over without trouble and gone his way. He had underestimated the capacity of the man in the dirty T-shirt to do him harm. An aging pimp, a Chink at that, what could he do even with the woman to help him? Well, he had seen what the man could do now. He must have had the cord or the wire or whatever it was ready to hand. And he knew how to use it, no doubt about that. Maybe he'd had a lot of practice.

But it was not over yet. What was that saying? The show isn't over till the fat woman sings? Well, he had heard no fat woman singing; only a scraggy old whore who was still wriggling under him like she was trying to get away but couldn't because she was trapped between him and the mattress. What a way to go! Sure, what a way to go!

He kicked backwards with the heel of his right foot and caught his assailant on the shin. The man made a sound as though he had drawn his breath in sharply. Crane would have given a lot to be able to draw a breath of any kind; it could have been a life-saver. But the unrelenting pressure of the ligature on his windpipe ruled that out. The kick had done nothing to loosen the man's grip, and the thing around his throat, that unwanted and deadly necklace, seemed to be biting ever more deeply. His eyes were popping; his tongue protruded. He was in agony.

This is the end, he thought. Sure as fate this is how it all ends. Curtains for Walter.

And after this he thought no more. Because he had been right, dead right, and that was what it was: Curtains for Walter. Curtains for Crane.

It was indeed one hell of a way to go.

3
Mr Chan

When another day had passed and still Crane had not returned to the ship Gregg became more and more worried about him. He paid another visit to the police station but got very little in the way of encouragement there. The sergeant he had spoken to before was polite but unhopeful. Gregg got the impression that he doubted whether the bosun was still alive, though no body fitting the description of Walter Crane had turned up. Apparently corpses were fished out of the water now and then, and if a likely one put in an appearance Gregg would certainly be informed. Meanwhile—

Meanwhile Gregg consulted with his chief officer, Frank Loder, and between them they came to the conclusion that it would be wise to start looking for a replacement for Walter Crane.

'I don't think he's coming back,' Loder said. 'If he'd simply drunk himself legless and was holed up somewhere getting over it he'd have sobered up by now and would have crawled back home.'

'That's true. So you think we should write him off?'

'Don't you?'

'Maybe so.'

'And we can't hang around in the hope that he'll suddenly put in an appearance. As soon as we're ready to sail we'll need to be on our way.'

Gregg had to agree with that. Keeping a ship in port longer than was necessary was a sure way of losing money, much as it might be pleasing to those members of the crew who were always glad of the opportunity to get ashore and savour the varied delights that were unavailable while at sea.

'Right then. We'd better look around for a replacement.'

'And if Crane does pop up all alive and kicking?'

'Just too bad for him. He'll have lost his job. But somehow I don't think he will. I'd say we've seen the last of that joker.'

With the help of an agent they found a new bosun with very little delay. He was a man of about forty, black-haired, round-faced, cheerful, with a ready grin that revealed a mouthful of pretty good teeth. He had the necessary credentials and he was immediately available.

His name was Tommy Chan.

Loder wondered whether it was a good idea to have a Chinese bosun.

'Why not?' Gregg asked.

'Might cause friction with the crew, don't you think?'

'Damn the crew. If Chan knows his job it seems to me immaterial what colour his skin is or how high his cheekbones are or how slit-eyed he is. We're hiring him to do a job, not win a male beauty contest.'

'Maybe so, but—'

'Anyway, he's available and we haven't time to stick around

waiting for a British bosun. They're not exactly thick on the ground in this part of the world.'

'That's so.'

'I think our Mr Chan will do very nicely. If not we shall have to try again.'

And that was that.

Chan came originally from Hong Kong and he spoke English pretty well. Gregg thought he was lucky to find such a man so quickly. It meant they could leave Singapore just as soon as the cargo was loaded and the hatches battened down.

There was the question of Crane's kit, which was still on board; but this did not amount to much and it was easily packed into the old battered suitcase in which he had carried it. This they left with the agent to hand over to its owner if he did eventually turn up.

Gregg knew of no one in England who ought to be informed of Crane's disappearance. It was common knowledge that he was separated from his wife, and he appeared to be something of a loner. Besides, it was not as if there was any certainty regarding his fate. If it had been known that he was dead the situation would have been different. As it was, nothing was known for certain except that he had gone missing.

The crew did not take at all kindly to the idea of having a Chinese bosun telling them what to do. There was a sense of grievance. It seemed to be felt that one of them might well have been promoted to the job vacated by Walter Crane. This was confided to the third mate, Harry Park; and he relayed it to the captain.

'They seem rather upset about it, sir.'

'Upset!' Gregg said. 'What right have they to be upset? If there was one of that lot worth promoting maybe I'd have done it. But there's not, and that's the truth of it. Scum, Mr Park. Moaning Minnies. One of them as bosun! Not on this ship.'

'Do you want me to tell them that, sir?'

Gregg looked hard at the young man. 'Now, Mr Park,' he said, 'would I be correct in assuming that you regard yourself as a reasonably intelligent person?'

Park shifted uneasily under Gregg's stare. 'Well, yes, sir.'

'So do I really need to tell you what to say to the crew? Bearing in mind that right now we're stuck with the bastards and don't want to make them more discontented than they already are. Do I, Mr Park?'

'No, sir. I suppose not.'

'Of course you do,' Gregg said. And then he grinned suddenly, as if to take the sting out of anything he had said. 'In my opinion, Mr Park, you have the makings of a first class ship's officer.'

'Well, thank you, sir.' Park managed to look surprised and gratified and a shade embarrassed all at the same time.

Gregg himself might have been surprised if he had known with what admiration the young man regarded him. To Park it seemed that his captain possessed all the qualities that he feared were lacking in himself. Gregg was his model; indeed, his hero; an ideal to be emulated if that were at all possible. He doubted whether he would ever be capable of doing so. But he would try. Yes, he would certainly try.

Besides the matter of the new bosun, the crew had another cause for some discontent. When the *W. H. Davies* left Singapore with a mixed cargo she headed for Surabaya in Java, and from Surabaya she proceeded to Davao in the Philippine island of

Mindanao. Next she sailed northward, heading for Taiwan; and still Gregg gave no indication that the ship would soon be returning to home waters. Indeed, it had all along been his intention to engage in the Far East trade, not only because of a feeling that it might prove more profitable for a tramp, but also because it had a romantic appeal to him.

He had discussed the matter with Loder and had found him in favour of the idea.

'Sounds okay to me,' Loder said. 'I've got no pressing engagements back in England.'

'And it doesn't have to be for ever. Depends on how things go. We'll just wait and see.'

'That's the beauty of it, isn't it? You never know what may be coming up next.'

'So you have no regrets about coming into partnership with me?'

'Are you kidding? Best move I ever made. This is the life for me.'

'Some people might say we're both of us crazy. We'll never get rich at this game, you know.'

'So who wants to be rich?'

Gregg laughed. 'Most people, I'd say. Why else would the lotteries do such good business?'

'Ah well, maybe a million or two would be nice. But it's just a dream, isn't it? Except for the few.'

Gregg spoke to the bosun about the report that there was discontent among the seamen. 'Have you heard any complaints?'

'What sort of complaints, Captain?' Chan asked.

'About being too long in this part of the world. Wanting to get back to England.'

'Oh, that.' Chan gave his white-toothed grin. 'Maybe some guys homesick. What they expect? You run a ship for their convenience? Take no notice, Captain. Seamen, they always got something to gripe about. If not one thing, then another. Don't listen. Not worth bothering your head about, those bastards.'

Gregg got the impression that Mr Chan had no very high opinion of British seamen. No love lost on either side could possibly best describe the relationship between bosun and deck crew. Not perhaps the best state of affairs for the making of a happy ship, but one that had to be accepted, at least for the present.

So with this festering sore at the heart of the ship, the *W. H. Davies* continued on her northward voyage and came in due course to the Luzon Strait. And it was here, in this island-dotted stretch of water between the northern extremity of the island of Luzon and the southernmost shore of Taiwan that the incident occurred.

4
Incident

It happened in the morning watch soon after one bell had sounded; at four thirty-five a.m. by the clock. Loder, as first mate, was on duty on the bridge, and Gregg, waking early and finding further sleep elusive, went up to join him.

It was a warm, clear night with no moon but a host of glittering stars which were reflected in an almost dead calm sea. Gazing forward it was possible to discern the shadowy outline of the forecastle and a white glimmer of foam where the bows sliced into the water like a plough drawing a furrow in the soil. Where the water slid past the ship's sides phosphorescence glowed, as though the sea itself had been set alight and was ready to burst into flame.

At the wheel, silent, almost motionless in the execution of his duty of keeping the vessel on course, was one of the discontented seamen; a lanky, skinny man who seemed to be all knees and elbows. He was a cockney from London's East End, and he had in fact been born in that part of dockland to which the ships no longer came.

His name was Stanley Briggs.

'This,' Loder remarked, 'is very peaceful, don't you think?'

'Very.'

'Difficult to imagine all the killing and maiming and general mayhem that's going on in various parts of the world right now. Why do people have to do it?'

'Human nature. Greed, envy, religious bigotry, intolerance of anyone with different views, different coloured skin, lust for money or power or someone else's wife. It's all been going on since man came down from the trees; and maybe before that. I guess it'll continue as long as there are men and women to carry on the tradition.'

'It's so senseless. With all the natural disasters there are: floods, hurricanes, tornadoes, earthquakes, volcanic eruptions, tidal waves, famine and so on, not to mention diseases of various kinds such as aids, malaria, cholera and good old-fashioned plague, you'd think people would have enough commonsense not to make more for themselves, wouldn't you?'

'Yes, you would.'

'So why do they do it?'

'Like I said, it's human nature. It'll never change.'

'And that,' Loder said with a laugh, 'is a pretty gloomy conclusion to reach on such a beautiful night as this.'

'Morning,' Gregg said. 'Don't you know this is the morning watch?'

'It's still dark. For my money that makes it night.'

'Have it your own way,' Gregg said. 'Night or morning, it's all very nice and peaceful.'

It was about two minutes later when they heard the sound. At first it was scarcely audible above the steady beat of the diesels that came throbbing up from the engine-room. But gradually it became louder, so that finally there could be no doubt what it was.

'A motor-boat,' Loder said. 'Can't be anything else.'

The wheelhouse was open on each side to allow a movement of cooling air to flow through, and the two men stepped out on to the starboard wing of the bridge. From there it became clear that the sound was coming from somewhere in the darkness astern.

'Now what,' Gregg said, 'would a motor-boat be doing out here at this time?'

Loder could provide no answer to that.

'And where has it come from?'

'One of the islands perhaps.'

This was a possibility. There were plenty of small islands between Luzon and Taiwan: the Babuyans and the Batans; both groups part of the Philippine archipelago.

'It's getting closer,' Loder said.

And that was when Gregg remembered something he had been told or had read concerning piracy in this part of the world. He had not thought much about it at the time, but now he began to wonder whether something of the kind might not be about to happen, with the *W. H. Davies* as the target. It was not a happy thought.

He walked to the extremity of the wing and looked towards the stern, but could make out very little in the darkness; and though the motor-boat could be heard, nothing of it was visible. It was showing no lights, and that in itself was odd, not to say ominous. Soon the engine note was so loud that the boat had to be very close to the ship.

Then suddenly another sound made itself heard. It was a kind of clang, as of metal striking metal, clearly audible to the two men on the bridge.

'What the devil was that?' Loder said.

Gregg did not answer, but the thought came into his head that a grapnel thrown upward from a boat and hooking itself to the bulwark might make just such a clanging sound. And if this was a correct guess regarding the origin of the noise there might already be men swarming up the rope attached to the grapnel and jumping down from the bulwark to the afterdeck of the ship. But still nothing was clearly visible in the gloom, though perhaps there was a vague shape that might have been the outline of a boat. Hard to tell for certain.

He said: 'I think we're being boarded.'

'Bloody hell!' Loder said. And he too peered into the darkness, seeking for confirmation of that sinister possibility. 'What do we do now?'

It was a question that Gregg had already asked himself. If pirates were in fact coming aboard, what could be done to repel them? They would most certainly be armed, and the only firearm on board the ship was a rather old revolver which was at that moment locked away in a safe in his cabin.

Finally he said: 'You stay here. I'm going to investigate.'

'Well, take care.'

'I intend to,' Gregg said. But he knew that taking care might not be enough. If armed men were coming on board they would have easy pickings, for it would be out of the question to resist them. 'Don't worry.'

Which, in the circumstances he reflected, was a pretty stupid thing to say. Because there was plenty to worry about, that was for sure. It had all been so peaceful until then; but now the peace looked like being broken. Well, so be it. What must be would be.

He made a move in the direction of the ladder leading down to the deck below, and as he reached it he heard the rapid patter of feet and knew that someone was running towards the bridge. He paused and saw the shadowy figure of a man coming up the ladder, another close behind him. In a moment the first man had reached the top.

'Back!' he snapped; and he pushed something hard into Gregg's chest. 'Back!'

Gregg stepped back very smartly, since it took no great power of perception to realize that the thing that was pressing into his chest was the muzzle of a gun, and this was giving his ribs a pretty hard time. The man followed him, keeping up the pressure; and now that he was in the faint light coming from the wheelhouse Gregg could see that he was a short, thickset character with a round face, high cheekbones and black hair. It was a reasonably safe bet that he was a Filipino. He was dressed in black trousers and a black shirt, canvas shoes on his feet; and the weapon he was pressing into Gregg's ribs was a submachine-gun, small but obviously lethal. Gregg was no expert on guns, but he thought it might be an Uzi. Whatever it was, he wished it were somewhere else; where it was it gave him a queasy feeling in the stomach, even though it was the chest it was prodding.

'Who are you? What do you want?' he demanded.

The man did not answer either question. Two other men had followed him up the ladder, both dressed as he was and probably Filipinos also. They were also armed, but with pistols. One of them moved up close to Loder, no doubt to ensure that he did nothing heroic, like trying to take the submachine-gun from the first man. It would have been a stupid thing to do, and Loder had shown no inclination to make any such attempt. When you were facing men with guns a knowledge of judo was not a great deal of use; you were likely to get a bullet in your flesh before you could really get to work. Loder was very well aware of this and was staying passive.

The man with the Uzi – if it was an Uzi – took the muzzle out of Gregg's ribs and gestured with it towards the wheelhouse.

'In there! Move!'

Gregg moved. He went into the wheelhouse and the man followed close behind. The other Filipinos came in too, bringing Loder with them. Briggs took one glance at all this unexpected company, saw the guns, gave a yelp and almost collapsed with fright. He released his grip on the wheel and made a move as if with the intention of making a quick exit on the port side of the wheelhouse.

Gregg put a stop to that by snarling at him: 'Stay where you are! Get back to the wheel, damn you! You could get a bullet in the back, you fool.'

The man with the Uzi said: 'You right, Captain. You tell him he better have sense. Where he go? Ship like prison. No escape.'

He spoke pretty good English, and he had guessed that Gregg was the captain. But it was an easy deduction from the epaulettes on the white shirt. This man obviously knew their significance.

Briggs took hold of the wheel again, but his hands were shaking. It was evident that the sight of three marauders armed with guns had scared the wits out of him.

Gregg spoke to the man with the Uzi, who appeared to be the leader. 'What do you want? There's no treasure on board this ship, if that's what you're looking for. We're carrying a mixed cargo. You like Manila hemp? Got some of that.'

All three of them gave a laugh at that. So it seemed they all knew enough English to get the gist of what he had said. But there was a certain mockery in the laughter which he did not like.

'You think we fools?' the Uzi man said. It was his leadership perhaps that gave him the privilege of carrying the submachine-gun. 'Cargo no interest to us.' He snapped his fingers. 'That for your damn cargo.'

Gregg hardly needed to ask what they were interested in. Cash would be the number one item; after that anything of value small enough to be easily carried away: cameras, binoculars, radios, rings, watches; the stuff that burglars went for on dry land. These men were burglars too; it was only the field of their operation that was different.

As if to confirm this surmise, the Uzi man said: 'Where you keep money?'

'What money?'

It was the wrong thing to say. It made the man angry. He showed his anger by jabbing Gregg in the chest with the muzzle of the gun hard. It hurt. It hurt a lot. It could have cracked a rib.

'You think you clever? But not so damn clever, hey? You want I shoot you in hand maybe? Just to teach you not be smart with me. So now no more smart stuff, hey? You got that?'

'I've got it,' Gregg said. His ribs were telling him that. 'You want money.'

'Damn right. You got money?'

'Some. Not much.'

'Not much, hey? Well, we see. I think now we go to captain's cabin. Maybe find some there.'

He turned to one of the others and said something that seemed to be in Spanish. Gregg had a smattering of that language and gathered that he was telling the man to stay in the wheelhouse and keep an eye on the helmsman.

'Now, Captain, let's go.'

Gregg shrugged. There was no point in making any protest. A

refusal to co-operate would have been met with instant violence, and the outcome would have been the same anyway. The men with guns were in control and had to be obeyed.

'This way then.'

He walked out of the wheelhouse with the Uzi man close at his heels. Loder and his minder followed. Briggs was left with the third member of the gang for company. He looked far from happy with this arrangement, but he had no choice.

The *W. H. Davies* stayed on course and forged ahead at her steady rate of knots as though nothing untoward were taking place within her superstructure. And the stars shone as brightly as before.

5

Cold Steel

They came to the captain's cabin and went inside and Gregg switched the light on. There was a fair amount of room in there, and among other fittings there was a safe. There was a desk up against one side and the safe was next to it. It was not disguised in any way; it was a pretty old-fashioned piece of work and it was really not much more than a steel locker. A professional safe-breaker could have opened it with a toothpick, but where would you find a safe-breaker on board a tramp ship?

The Uzi man noticed it at once. 'Ah!' he said. 'So that's where the valuables are kept.'

'There are no valuables,' Gregg said. 'What do you think this is? A luxury passenger liner?'

There were in fact two cabins for the accommodation of passengers on board the *W. H. Davies*, but they had never been occupied since Gregg and Loder had become owners of the vessel. They tended to become dumps for junk that had no other home. Maybe some day someone would turn up needing to be taken somewhere, but it seemed unlikely. A tramp with no regular itinerary was not in the business of attracting passengers.

'Is it locked?'

'Yes, of course it's locked.'

'Why?'

'What do you mean, why?'

'Nothing much in it, why lock it?'

'Because it's a safe. That's what you do with safes. You lock them.'

'With nothing inside?'

'Yes. With nothing inside.'

It sounded pretty thin, Gregg thought. As thin as a starved greyhound. And he could see that he might as well have saved his breath, because the man was not buying it. He was not buying it and he was getting impatient too.

'Open it,' he said. And he made a threatening gesture with the gun.

It was the gun that bothered Gregg. It was so small and yet so deadly. A thing like that could bring your life to a sudden and sticky end, leaving no more to be enjoyed. And he wanted more; he was not ready to go to his long home yet, and he would not be ready for quite a while.

Now that he could see the man more clearly in the brighter light of the cabin he liked the look of him even less. And the liking had been close to zero right from the start. This character seemed a nasty piece of work at best, and what made things worse for him in the beauty stakes was a livid scar which stretched from the left jawbone in a slanting line to a rather lower point on the right side of his neck. It looked as though some ill-disposed person had at one time in the past attempted to slit his throat and had done a botched job. Which, to Gregg's way of thinking was a great pity.

When the man ordered him to open the safe he thought for a moment of saying that this was impossible because the key had been lost. But on second thoughts he decided not to try anything in that line because there was not the slightest chance of its being believed. The man with the scarred neck was not as gullible as that, and it would simply make him more impatient and maybe goad him into doing a bit more work with the gun, like shooting him in the hand, as he had already threatened to do.

So again Gregg gave a shrug and pulled out a drawer in the desk where the key was kept. And then he unlocked the safe and opened it.

'Ah!' the man said. And he shouldered Gregg away and started rooting around inside.

There was in fact more money in the safe than Gregg had suggested. He found it convenient to keep some cash handy, chiefly in American dollars, which were acceptable in most parts of the world. The man with the scarred neck was not long in finding this little lot, and he gave a grunt of satisfaction.

'Now here is something. I think here is more than you say. I think is quite a lot, hey?'

He put the submachine-gun down on the floor and started transferring the cash to a large canvas bag slung over his shoulder by a leather strap. The other man had a similar bag, obviously for carrying away any loot that might be picked up.

It did not take long for the man with the scarred neck to transfer all the cash from the safe to his bag. He did not bother to count it; there would be time for that later, It irked Gregg to see his money going into the bag. It might not have been a fortune, but he was not so rich that he could afford to lose even that amount. And even if he had been a Croesus he would have resented being robbed by a damned water thief.

He felt an impulse to take advantage of this moment while the man had laid down his weapon to have a go at him, perhaps using one of those judo tricks that Loder had taught him. Or maybe he could grab the Uzi – if it was an Uzi – and use it to turn the tables on its owner. But he knew that this could not be done in a moment, and there was the other man to reckon with. He had a big black self-loading pistol in his hand and might not be slow to use it when he saw what was going on. So all that was likely to be accomplished by any move of the kind envisaged would be a bullet in some vulnerable part of the body. Which meant any part at all as far as he was concerned.

So he got no further than thinking about this kind of heroic act, because heroism was all very well in its place, but this maybe was not the place and it was not worth risking your life or maybe a non-lethal bullet wound for a few stinking American dollars – or even for a lot of the same if it came to that.

And soon the man with the scarred neck completed the transfer of the cash from the safe to his canvas bag; and then he picked up the submachine-gun and the moment of possibly taking action against him had passed.

'Satisfied?' Gregg inquired. 'You going to leave us now?'

It was all so bizarre, he thought. One could hear the steady beat of the engines propelling the vessel on its way, and in the engine-room there would be men at work, oblivious to what was taking place in this cabin above their heads. Other men would be asleep in their bunks, never dreaming of anything as unlikely as piracy on the high seas, perpetrated by a modern breed of buccaneer. Yet it was happening; there was no getting away from the fact, unpalatable as it might be.

The man ignored the question. He said: 'You got watch. Give me.'

Gregg was wearing a wristwatch, and it was not a cheap one.

It had cost him more than two hundred pounds, and he hated to part with it. But the gun was threatening him again and he knew that any argument would be pointless.

'Damn you!' he said. But he unstrapped the wristwatch and handed it to the man, who glanced at it and put it in his pocket.

Loder also had a watch on his wrist, and it was a more valuable one than Gregg's. It was a Rolex which had been a gift from a wealthy aunt. Giving it up must have been as painful as having a tooth extracted without anaesthetic. But he had no choice. The man who was holding the pistol, a rather skinny individual with prominent teeth, took it from him and pocketed it.

'So now you really will be going, I suppose,' Gregg said.

The man with the scar gave a jeering laugh. 'You think we finish now? Not yet. Plenty room in bags to fill.'

He took another look inside the safe and found the revolver. He held it up for the other man to see, and they both had a laugh. Evidently they were contemptuous of this old weapon. But it went in the bag nevertheless.

Once more Gregg had that impulse to tackle the man, take him off balance, snatch the gun from him. If he could count on Loder to act at the same time they might between them pull it off. But how could he make a signal to Loder, give him warning of what was in his mind? If they did not act in unison there would be no hope of the move succeeding and they would only make trouble for themselves; bad trouble. And yet, to let the bastards get away with it and not lift a finger to prevent them; that was a bitter pill to swallow.

The man with the scar seemed to read his mind. 'You think you maybe try something? Think maybe turn tables, hey? Forget it, Captain. All you get for trouble is bullet in you. And that nasty. Hurt like hell. Maybe kill. You wanna be kill?'

Gregg did not want to be killed and he did not want a bullet in him. There were occasions when you could not win, when you had to accept defeat with as much grace as it was possible to muster. This was one of those occasions.

He had just come to this unpleasant conclusion when the door burst open and Mr Chan stepped into the cabin.

'What goes?' Chan asked.

He spoke softly, even politely, but the question was unnecessary. He could see perfectly well what went. He knew it, Gregg knew it, Loder knew it, and the men with the guns knew it. Yet Mr Chan seemed to feel obliged to ask the question, as though it were an essential preliminary to all that was to follow.

'What goes?'

No one felt obliged to answer. Instead, the man with the scar made a move to raise the muzzle of the Uzi gun and point it at the bosun with the intention perhaps of making some holes in his very solid body. But Chan was far too quick for him. Before the barrel of the gun could come to bear on him his right hand made a movement so swift it was difficult to follow it with the eye, and something flew from the hand, something that glittered in the lamplight, and in a moment there was a knife imbedded in the right shoulder of the man with the scar.

Gregg had not seen the knife in the bosun's hand. Perhaps it had been hidden behind his back; but it had been there somewhere, and it had been thrown with speed and accuracy by a man who was certainly no novice at that game. This came as a revelation to Gregg, for Chan had made no mention of this ability when signing on. But no doubt he had seen no reason to do so, since it was not an accomplishment normally required of a seaman. However, no one could deny that on this occasion it had come in remarkably handy.

The man with the scar gave a cry of pain and dropped the submachine-gun, and Gregg quickly picked it up.

Meanwhile, the skinny man had made a move with his pistol, evidently with the intention of shooting Mr Chan. But he never got to the point of actually firing the gun, because another man took a hand in the game and prevented him from even pressing the trigger. This other man was the ship's cook, who, like Chan, was a Hong Kong Chinese. His name was John Lee, a fat, jovial person from whom Gregg would never have expected anything in the way of physical violence. Possibly on this occasion he felt that something in that line was called for, and he had certainly come well prepared. He had entered the cabin behind Chan, and his chosen weapon was somewhat different from the bosun's but equally effective. It was not a knife but a meat cleaver, probably as sharp as a razor. With it Mr Lee made a quick chopping movement and the blade came down on the skinny man's wrist, the one which was attached to the hand that held the pistol.

It was possible that Lee had not been trying his hardest; if he had been, the hand might have become completely detached, but as it was the detachment was only partial. The skinny man screamed and blood spurted. The pistol fell to the floor and Mr Chan scooped it up.

He looked at Gregg and grinned. 'Now, Captain,' he said, 'I think we taken care of these bloody buggers.'

The adjective was a fitting one, Gregg thought; there was certainly plenty of blood flowing. And it was also certain that the bosun and the cook had arrived in the nick of time. Before that the situation had looked sticky indeed. He wondered just how it had come about. It had certainly been no accident, for it was hardly likely that the two men would have been wandering around at that hour – or any hour for that matter – armed with cold steel in the shape of a large knife and a cleaver if they had had no set purpose in mind.

But it was not the time for explanations. So all he said was: 'Yes, bosun, I think you have.'

6
Weapons

Bosun Chan was by habit an early riser. He liked to be out and about before the rest of the crew was stirring. John Lee rose early because his duties on board made it essential; he had to get things moving in the galley well before breakfast time. There Chan would find him in company with the galley boy, another Chinese, considerably younger than his superior and far thinner.

Mr Chan, being on friendly terms with the cook, would call in at the galley for a chat and a mug of tea and a smoke. He found it a pleasant way of starting the day's routine.

On this particular morning he had not been there for long when they all heard the sound of the approaching motor-boat. The galley being at the after end of the accommodation amidships and at a lower level than the bridge, Chan and Lee and the galley boy were able to hear the sound rather more clearly than the captain and the mate. And it was Chan who was immediately suspicious, because he had had previous experience of piracy in waters not far distant from those in which the *W. H. Davies* was now making her way.

He confided his suspicions to the cook and suggested that they should take certain precautions, the first of which was to switch off the light in the galley. The door was standing open to let in the cool morning air, and Chan stepped over the high sill and peered down aft in the direction from which the sound was coming. It came nearer, growing steadily louder until it seemed to be very close indeed. Then it suddenly became quieter, as though the engine had been throttled down; and immediately after that Chan heard the clang of the grapnel that had been heaved up to hook on to the bulwark.

Chan was on the port side of the deck, and he took a few steps aft to a point where he could gaze across to the starboard side, from which the sound was coming. He could see little in the gloom, but, he heard a patter of feet and in the faint starlight caught a glimpse of three shadowy figures flitting past in the direction of the bridge.

He went back into the galley and told Lee to switch the light on; which the cook did.

'They've gone towards the bridge. Three of them.'

'Three,' Lee said. 'Ah!'

'They'll be armed.'

'Yes.'

'They'll go for the best pickings first. Then they'll come to us and the crew.'

Lee nodded. 'It's the way.'

'Question is,' Chan said, 'do we let them?'

'Another question,' Lee said. 'Can we stop them?'

'I got things. I like to keep them. They're mine. The same with money.'

'Me too. I work hard for what I get. Damn bastards, those pirates. They don't work. Just steal from you and me. That's bad.'

'So you're with me? Do we let them get away with this? Like hell, we do.'

'I'm with you,' Lee said. 'But how we do it?'

Chan picked up one of the cook's knives. It had a long blade, of polished steel, wide at one end and tapering to a point. He held it in his hand as if gauging the weight, the balance.

'This is my weapon. Now choose yours.'

Lee took the cleaver from a hook and made a few passes with it. 'This is mine.'

'You want me to go with you?' the galley boy asked. He did not sound at all eager.

'No,' Lee said. 'You'd be in the way.'

The galley boy looked relieved. 'Okay then. I stay here. Get on with work.'

Chan and Lee had a brief conference and came to the conclusion that one of the first places the pirates would visit in the search for rich pickings would be the captain's cabin.

'So we go there?' Lee said.

'We go there.'

The door was slightly ajar when they arrived, and light was spilling out into the alleyway. They could hear voices inside but could not catch the words. One of the voices had a growling quality; there seemed to be a threat in it.

Chan looked at Lee, gave a lift of the eyebrows and whispered: 'Now?'

Lee nodded. 'Now.'

Chan kicked the door wide open and went in, holding the knife behind his back. Lee was at his heels. Chan took in at a glance what was going on. Nevertheless, he asked the question:

'What goes?'

The only answer he got was a movement from the man with the scarred neck, swinging the gun he was holding in Chan's direction. Chan did not wait for a challenge from the man; there was too much likelihood that it would be a case of shoot first and ask questions afterwards. So he brought the hand holding the cook's knife from behind his back and threw it.

He was pleased to see that he had lost none of his skill in the art of knife-throwing, which he had learned years ago, before taking to the seagoing life. It was true that the distance had been short and the target fairly large, but the result was highly satisfactory nevertheless. And then his friend Lee had chipped in with great efficiency also.

There remained one question to be answered. Where was the third man? He felt sure he had seen three when they came on board. And in a way it was fortunate that only two of them had been present in the cabin, since a third might have made things a shade more difficult. But he had not been there, and now, wherever he was, it should not be hard to deal with him, seeing how the odds had suddenly gone against him.

Chan looked at Gregg and grinned and said: 'Now, Captain, I think we taken care of these bloody buggers.'

And Gregg said: 'Yes, bosun, I think you have.'

But the job was not yet finished. Here were two Filipinos bleeding like stuck pigs and moaning not a little, besides making a fine mess of the cabin as well. The one with the scarred neck had made an effort to pull the knife out of his shoulder but had not succeeded. He was on his knees and looking sick. No doubt feeling as bad as he looked too. Chan walked across and did the job for him with a sharp wrench. It must have hurt like hell. He screamed and a lot more blood came out. Chan calmly wiped the blade of the knife on the man's shirt, which was rather like adding insult to injury.

'Well,' Gregg said, 'I think we'd better go and deal with the one on the bridge.'

'Ah!' Chan said. 'So that is where he is. I was sure there were three of the swine.'

Gregg looked surprised. 'You knew they were here?'

'Saw them come aboard. I am in the galley with cookie. We hear the boat and I go take a look. Damn good thing too.'

'No doubt about that,' Gregg said. And it occurred to him that there was much more to this bosun than he had ever suspected.

They left the cook to keep an eye on the two men in the cabin while the rest of them made their way to the bridge. Mr Lee with his cleaver was quite happy to watch over two pirates who were disarmed and badly injured.

'We'll not be long,' Gregg said.

The man on the bridge put up no resistance. When he saw them come into the wheelhouse, two with guns, the third with a bloodstained knife, he needed no telling just how drastically the situation had changed in favour of the opposition.

'Give me your gun,' Gregg said.

The man hesitated for a moment, but a gesture with the Uzi persuaded him and he handed it over. He seemed bewildered by this turn of events and no doubt was trying to figure out just how it had happened. He had seen his two comrades depart from the wheelhouse with the two unarmed ship's officers well and truly under their orders. Yet now, here were those same two officers back again, themselves armed and accompanied by a seaman with a bloodstained knife. How could it have happened? The blood on the knife was a clue, but not a full explanation. His bewilderment was therefore understandable.

Able Seaman Stanley Briggs, still at the wheel, heard the three men enter the wheelhouse and glanced over his shoulder at them. He too was amazed, but in his case the amazement was mixed with a great feeling of relief. He had not enjoyed his session with the gunman for sole company. Reason might have told him that the man was unlikely to shoot him, since it was in the best interests of the man and his compatriots that the ship should be kept on course, and who else was there to do this than the helmsman, one Stanley Briggs as ever was? But Briggs was a coward, and the mere presence of a criminal with a gun casting an eye on him and almost breathing down his neck was enough to keep him terrified and in fear of his life for the entire period of time between the departure of the captain and the mate under armed guard and their utterly unexpected return several minutes later, themselves now armed and in the company of Bosun Chan. Boy, was he glad to see them! Even though he detested Tommy Chan and had no love for any ship's officer as a matter of principle.

'Are you okay, Briggs?' Gregg inquired.

'Yessir,' Briggs answered.

'You've had no trouble?'

'No, sir.'

Only the trouble of having to do his job with a bloody maniac with a gun at his back. Only the trouble of having to stick it out up here at the wheel, not knowing what was going on elsewhere and what would be the end of it all. Oh no, sir! No trouble at all, thank you very much, sir! And all this when the ship ought never to have been in these waters anyway. It was not what he had signed on for. Not bloody likely. Pirates indeed! You didn't get them in the civilised parts of the world. Only out here in the Far East, in amongst all these sodding islands. It was not good enough, not good enough at all.

Gregg, unaware of the thoughts that were passing in Briggs's mind, unaware of the anger and resentment that possessed him now that the terror had passed; feelings that were perhaps the direct result of that previous fear which he knew had been observed by the captain and had led to a rebuke from him; Gregg, unaware of all this said:

'Well, it's all over now. Mr Loder will be staying on the bridge with you for the rest of the watch, so you'll have nothing more to worry about. All right?'

'All right,' Briggs said. 'Sir.'

And thank you very much, sir, for nothing. Thank you very much for getting us into this kind of trouble. Wait till he told the rest of the lads what had happened, and how they might have been robbed and even had their throats slit while they were asleep in their bunks. They were unhappy enough already, just as he was; but now they would be even more unhappy when they heard the full story of that piracy attempt in the morning watch. Because the same thing might occur in the future with far more unpleasant results if the *W. H. Davies* continued trading around these bloody Pacific islands. Oh yes, he would tell them all right. Bet your sweet life, he would.

The man with the scarred neck and his henchman were both sitting on the floor when Gregg and Chan returned to the cabin, bringing the third man with them. The two wounded men were still bleeding and appeared to be in a pretty bad way. Gregg wanted them off the ship as soon as possible, but it was obvious that they would need some help and it would be as well to stop some of that bleeding if at all possible.

Carrying out his instructions, Chan and Lee did some rough bandaging with a torn up sheet; and then, with the third man giving a hand, they were helped to their feet and taken back to the boat from which they had come. This was still moving along with the ship, its engine running and fenders made from old motor tyres hanging between it and the hull. The grapnel was still hooked on to the bulwark and the lower end of the rope was secured to a cleat at the bows of the boat.

It was quite a sizeable motor-launch and there was a fourth man in it, waiting for the return of the others. It must have been a nasty shock to him when he saw in what condition two of them now were. It was apparent to Gregg that these two, each with only one useful arm, could never make the descent to the launch by means of the rope, so he sent the bosun to fetch a Jacob's ladder to hang over the side. This was soon brought and fixed in place, and then the two men were helped to descend it to the deck of the boat. During this operation the fourth pirate was jabbering away at the others, apparently demanding to be told just what had happened. He was getting little in the way of answers, and what he did get seemed to please him not at all; which was hardly surprising. He would certainly not be receiving a share of any lucrative pickings, since there were none. Gregg and Loder had recovered their wristwatches, and the cash and revolver had been returned to the safe. In fact the entire operation as far as the pirate gang was concerned had been a complete disaster.

'What we do with the guns?' Chan asked. He had the two pistols stuck in his belt, while Gregg was carrying the submachine-gun, which on examination had proved to be indeed an Uzi. 'We keep them?'

'No,' Gregg said. 'Chuck them overboard.' He handed the Uzi to Chan.

'Good gun,' Chan said, looking thoughtfully at the weapon in his hand. 'Sure you don't want to keep it?'

'Quite sure. Throw it away. The pistols too. And make sure our friends in the boat see you do it. We haven't got any ammunition for them anyway.'

'They loaded, Captain.'

'Maybe they are. Makes no difference. Get rid of them.'

Chan shrugged. 'Okay, Captain. That what you want, okay.'

He moved to the bulwark, looked down on the men in the launch and shouted: 'Ahoy there! You forgot your guns.'

They all looked up at him and he showed them the weapons in his hands.

'Catch!'

He gave a mocking laugh and dropped them one by one into the sea. They made three splashes and were gone. The men in the launch watched impassively. Two of them could not at that moment have cared less about the loss of three guns. They had bigger troubles.

Chan took his seaman's knife from the pigskin sheath at the back of his belt and slashed the rope attached to the grapnel. It parted and that link between launch and ship was severed. A few minutes later the smaller craft had disappeared from sight.

The incident was finished.

7
Poison

'Strictly speaking,' Loder observed, 'I suppose we ought to have slung the bastards in the brig and handed them over to the authorities when we reached port.'

'You think the Taiwanese would have thanked us for that?' Gregg asked. 'Even if it had been at all practical.'

'Maybe not.'

'It's not their pigeon.'

'So whose is it? Ours?'

'Maybe.'

'Are you going to do anything about it?'

'I don't think there's anything I can do. I'll enter it in the log and that'll be the end of it.'

'And they get away scot-free.'

'Not entirely. Two of them certainly wouldn't think so. And they lost the guns and went away empty-handed. They'll really be sore about that.'

'So let's just hope we don't get that lot on board again. Next time they might start shooting straightaway.'

'Maybe so. But it's unlikely to happen. This could be our last time in these waters.'

'That's true,' Loder said.

He had finished his watch some hours earlier. It was now broad daylight and news of what had occurred during the morning watch when most of the ship's company were asleep or at work in the engine-room was being passed around by those who had taken part in the incident or had heard about it from those who had. In this process some of the story had become a little garbled, but the essential facts regarding the encounter with the pirates remained. There was certainly blood on the floor of the captain's cabin, and it was general knowledge now that this blood had been shed by two of the men who had boarded the ship from a launch and had been somewhat cut about by the bosun and the cook, wielding respectively a knife and a cleaver.

These two heroes themselves seemed inclined to make light of what they had done, but the fact remained that they had probably saved quite a number of their shipmates from being robbed. The gratitude of most of the seamen was somewhat muted because of their detestation of Mr Chan, but they had to admit that in this instance he had helped them all, even though his object had probably been only to help himself. The other part had been merely incidental, so they really owed him nothing.

Gregg had a talk with the man himself and got the full story of how he and the cook happened to appear so providentially on the scene when most urgently needed. He also asked about the knife-throwing.

'When did you learn that trick? Have you ever been in a circus act?'

Chan was cagey. He seemed reluctant to talk about it. 'No, Captain. No circus. I did a bit of it one time. Just for fun.'

'Well, you certainly haven't lost the knack. You were dead on target.'

'Luck, Captain, just luck. Knife could've gone anywhere.'

Gregg did not believe him. He believed that given the same kind of situation another time Chan would throw the knife as accurately again. And that kind of ability was not acquired without much practice, but he did not pursue the matter further. If Chan had his secrets he was entitled to keep them to himself.

Chan had in fact been sparing with the truth. He was very young when he first practised knife-throwing. He was one of a gang of kids in Hong Kong who modelled themselves on the Triads, which were so much a feature of the colony's criminal underworld at that time. Indeed, it was the ambition of practically all these tearaway youngsters to become eventually full members of a Triad themselves. In the end not all of them by any means did so. Some even grew out of this phase and developed into decent, law-abiding citizens. Others became petty criminals and were arrested and sent to jail with sickening frequency.

Chan became neither a petty criminal nor a solid citizen. He was spotted as likely material by a Triad talent scout and was taken into this secret society at a very early age.

He might have continued in it if it had not been for a woman. The woman's name was Molly Wang. She was twenty-five years old and Chan was nineteen. He was a good-looking young man and she took a fancy to him. Which might have been perfectly all right if she had not happened to be the girlfriend of one of the top men in the Triad. The man's name was Lui, and he was as hard and mean as they came. Anyone with the slightest regard for his own safety would have steered well clear of Molly, knowing that she was real poison and not to be taken at any price.

But she was also a beauty, and Chan at this time in his life was young enough to be easily seduced by a woman older than himself and much experienced in the way of the world. He was also a cocky youngster and didn't give a damn for the danger of running around with this particular one. It was not that he was unaware of her relationship with Lui; it was just that he did not care. He could look after himself. Or so he thought.

He was to discover that he was wrong about that. He was no longer dealing with kids of his own age or younger, who looked up to him as their leader. Now he was amongst men who were tougher even than he was. And maybe the toughest and meanest of them all was the man named Lui.

It did not take long for this man to get wind of what was going on, and he was not slow to take punitive action. Chan was beaten up and kicked out of the Triad with a warning not to be seen around any more if he valued his life. He remembered that beating long after. Some of it was with bamboo rods, and he had scars on his body to remind him. Scars in his mind too.

He hid himself away, like an animal licking its wounds; and when he had recovered he waited to take his revenge on Lui, the man who had had him whipped and had taken a leading part in the whipping. He stalked the man for weeks, and one night he caught him off guard, alone and drunk in a narrow alleyway. He pushed him into an open doorway, dark and deserted.

'This for you, Lui,' he said.

And he stuck a knife into him and left him bleeding on the ground and walked away.

The next day he got a job as deckhand on board a small Portuguese ship that was leaving very shortly. The ship was old and rusty, a coal-burner with soot from the funnel on everything you touched; the crew slovenly and the officers little better. The captain was a fat, greasy man, bald as a coot, with a straggly moustache and a dark jowl. He took Chan on because the vessel was short-handed and it was difficult to attract good seamen to such a rattletrap of a ship. Moreover, he seemed to take an instant liking to the young man and disregarded the lack of experience which Chan made no attempt to disguise.

'You'll learn. If you don't we throw you overboard to the sharks to eat.'

Chan hoped it was a joke but could not be sure. A rumbling sound which seemed to come up from the region of Captain Costa's belly might have been a laugh.

Next day the ship left port with Chan on board. His shipmates were a mixed bunch, none very prepossessing. A few were ethnic Chinese from Macau, which the *Santa Paula* frequently visited. Chan was careful not to give offence to anyone and concealed his contempt for the lot of them with a show of friendliness. It was a wise policy, since it was from them he needed to learn this new trade.

He picked up the rudiments of seamanship very quickly and took to the sailor's life with remarkable aptitude. Rather to his own surprise, he liked it, despite the company he was forced to keep and the wretched quarters that quite literally stank. He soon decided that his future beckoned to him in this direction. The SS *Santa Paula* would be the first rung of the ladder and he would not remain on that rung for long.

And so it turned out. He became proficient. He moved from ship to ship. He rose in rank. At times he had visions of leaping over that invisible barrier between the upper and lower decks, but he knew in his heart that this was never on the cards. Yet, though he liked the life well enough, with its continual moving around the world and tasting the pleasures offered in a variety of ports, it was not enough; he wanted more. The fact was that he was still at heart the young outlaw who had been a leader of the youthful gang in Hong Kong and had joined the Triad from which he had been so summarily dismissed. Even now he was hopeful that one day there would come the chance of making some real money, even if it had to be by criminal means. His had never been a true conversion from the old ways; and this might have been one reason why he had kept the polish on his skill with the knife.

He had returned to Hong Kong occasionally whenever a ship he was serving in chanced to visit that port. He had been wary at first of going ashore, though he doubted whether he was any longer in danger. In the course of one visit he encountered one of the members of the Triad to which he had once belonged. The man greeted him amicably enough and informed him that Lui was long dead.

'Had a knife stuck in him one night.'

'Ah!' Chan said.

'You didn't hear about that?'

'No.'

'They never found who did it.' The man gave Chan a searching look and grinned. 'Happened not long after you left us over that business with Molly. Sure you didn't hear about it?'

'Dead sure,' Chan said.

'Not that any of us was sorry to lose him. We never liked the pig.'

'No? I didn't either, to tell the truth.' And Chan gave a laugh. The other man laughed too. 'You had reason, as I recall.'

'What happened to Molly?' Chan asked.

'She's still around. Older.'

'She would be. So am I.'

'Not as pretty as she was.'

'No?'

'Because of the scars on her face.'

Chan said sharply: 'What scars?'

'What the big man made with a razor. Really spoiled her looks. You want to see her again?'

'No,' Chan said. 'I don't think I do.'

So more years had passed, and now he had the job of bosun on board the MV *W. H. Davies*. And still the big chance had not come up, and perhaps never would. Maybe he should have tried to get back into the Triads; but were they having such a good time under the new bosses, the People's Republic of China? He had heard not. He had even heard that some of them had moved to London and were carrying on their operations there. He did not know whether it was true or not. What could you believe?

Stanley Briggs was making much of his ordeal in having to stay at the wheel with an armed Filipino gunman breathing down his neck.

'I could've got a bullet in the back of my head any time.'

One of the seamen he was addressing remarked that this had not been likely. 'They wanted you to keep the ship on course, di'n't they?'

'Maybe and maybe not. Could've done me in soon's they'd got no more use for me. How was I to know?'

'Shakin' in your shoes, was you? Wettin' your pants, maybe?'

'Ah,' Briggs said, 'it's easy for you to laugh. You wasn't there. Snorin' in your bunks, all you lot. And I'll tell you this, you could've had your throats slit while you was asleep. Could've had your throats slit and all your cash and gear stole. How would you have liked that?'

This suggestion had some effect on them. It seemed that this possibility had not occurred to them until Briggs put it into their heads, and it did not please them.

Briggs noted this with satisfaction and went on with his complaint. 'We never oughter be in this part of the world. It ain't what I signed on for. Nor none of you neither, I'd say. Question is, when's our precious Captain Gregg going to put an end to this Far East lark and head for home? You tell me that.'

Nobody told him. Nobody knew the answer. And not knowing it, they were not happy.

8
Hero

The MV *W. H. Davies* stayed only a few days in Kaohsiung discharging part of the cargo and taking on more items. Gregg made no official report of the piracy incident. Why bother? The outcome had been satisfactory from his point of view, if not from that of the pirates. Without the timely intervention of the bosun and the cook a far less happy conclusion might have been reached; but as it was, the only regrettable consequence was some bloodstaining in his cabin which was proving difficult to erase completely. Things could have been much worse.

There was of course another result of the incident: it had added to the unrest in the crew; and he could not be unaware of this. Briggs was the worst of them, but they were all hankering for a voyage that would take them into home waters, and Gregg had to admit that they were not altogether unreasonable in entertaining this desire. He could see their point of view even though he had no intention of doing what they wished.

'If they don't like it,' he remarked to Loder, 'they'll just have to do the other thing.'

Loder himself was not altogether happy with this state of

things. He would have preferred to have a contented crew. But he did not argue. He just said: 'Well, I hope we don't get any more pirates coming aboard. Another time it might not end quite so satisfactorily. Can't always rely on the bosun to do his knife-throwing act.'

'That's so. I'm surprised it happened once. A bit of a mystery man, our Mr Chan, wouldn't you say?'

Loder agreed. 'But all Chinese are a mystery to me.'

'Well, mystery or not, he does his job well enough, and that's the main thing.'

'Yes,' Loder said, 'I suppose it is.'

But he did sometimes wonder what Tommy Chan might be hiding from them. He wondered about that quite a lot.

The business in Kaohsiung being completed, they left port and headed for Hong Kong. And the stay in Hong Kong was protracted by the necessity for certain work to be done on the engines.

It was also in Hong Kong that the deck crew decided to leave en bloc. Briggs, as spokesman for the other malcontents, informed Gregg of their decision.

'We've had enough. We want to go home.'

'And how do you propose to get home?' Gregg inquired.

'You leave that to us,' Briggs said. 'Just you pay us what's owing and that'll be that. We'll pack our things and go.'

'Are you sure you're doing the right thing?'

'Oh, we're sure all right.'

'And you won't change your minds?'

'Not unless you change yours about keeping the ship out here in this part of the world. Now if you was to promise to start heading back to England soon as the engines is patched up, we might agree to stay on. What do you say to that, Captain?'

Gregg was angered by the effrontery of the man. He answered rather sharply: 'Do you think this ship is run for your benefit?'

'Oh no,' Briggs said, and there was a sneer in his words. 'I know it ain't. That would be too much to expect. We all know who gets the benefit, don't we? You and Mr Loder; 'cause you and him's the owners, ain't you? You're the ones that's got the money and is getting rich from us poor sods as do the real work. Well, it ain't going on any longer. We ain't going to risk our necks with them bloody pirates just because you meanter keep the ship out here where the sods operate. It ain't good enough, and that's the truth of it, I'm telling you.'

'So you're telling me,' Gregg said; holding his temper in check under the goading of this man who really got under his skin. 'And if that's the way you feel, go and be damned to you.'

'It is the way I feel, and I ain't the only one. The others feel the same way. We're united in this.'

'Then good riddance to the lot of you.'

It occurred to him that if the crew had been union men Briggs would almost certainly have been the shop steward. But this was one of the advantages of sailing under that flag of convenience; there was no union to be dealt with.

'So be it then,' Briggs said.

He turned and left the cabin where the interview had taken place, and where the bloodstains were still faintly visible as a reminder to him – if such were needed – of that nocturnal visit that had scared the living daylights out of him.

Gregg was not sorry to see him go; he had never liked the man. But if the other seamen for whom he claimed to be speaking left also it would be annoying, to say the least. It meant that he would have to look for replacements, and these might not be easy to find. It was things like this which demonstrated that being both owner and captain of a ship was not without its drawbacks. There was no one to pass the buck to; it stopped with you.

He discovered later that the situation was not quite as bad as it might have been. The rot had not spread to any other sections of the ship's company. Chief Engineer Grimley had become such a misogynist after the defection of his wife Vera that he had no desire to go woman-hunting, and he cared little regarding what ports the ship visited. It was all one to him.

The second engineer, Clegg, might have been happier if the *W. H. Davies* had not spent so long a time in the Far East, but he was much too self-effacing to make any complaint on that score. This might have brought him into conflict with Arthur Grimley, and he lacked the courage to risk that. Besides which, he could think of little in England that called irresistibly to him to return. He had a wife, a thin, colourless woman with a nagging tongue and nothing about her that was any longer attractive to him. He often wondered why he had ever married her. It had been her suggestion of course, and he had not had the strength of will to resist. Why would he be eager to return to her? He sent her postcards from various ports of call, conveying in a minimum of words a love he did not feel.

As to those other troglodytes who laboured in the gloomy depths of the ship's hull, which reeked of engine oil and echoed with the thumping of the diesels and the occasional clanging of metal on metal, they said very little. Certainly they did not side with the deckhands, with whom they seemed to have nothing much in common. And possibly they reflected that there was a lot of unemployment back home in the United Kingdom and that they had steady jobs even if these did take them to distant seas. They might also have remembered the old saying: More days, more dollars. There was truth in that.

The carpenter was a kind of odd man out, and he was not at all inclined to ally himself with Briggs and his associates. Alfred Swain was a hulking, round-shouldered, middle-aged man who might have seemed awkward and clumsy but could work wonders with a piece of wood and the tools of his trade, handling them with the expertise of a skilled surgeon. He was taciturn, and if he had any opinions on the various subjects that came up for discussions in the seamen's mess he kept them very much to himself, answering any direct question with no more than a sardonic smile, as if to indicate that he had far too much sense to allow himself to be drawn into any argument of that description.

A good deal of his spare time he spent lying on his bunk reading paperback novels and other books that he borrowed from the ship's small library. When he ventured ashore he went alone, and would occasionally return drunk and a trifle unsteady on his legs, but taciturn as ever.

The two stewards were more outgoing; they would talk to anyone on any subject. They were both rather plump, sleek men, dark-haired and cleanshaven. They would go ashore whenever they got the chance and seemed to have no burning desire to get back to England. Gregg suspected that they enjoyed certain delights which were more freely available in Oriental ports than they were on their native soil. But this was none of his business, and he had no desire to know how they diverted themselves when away from the ship. His only concern was that they should carry out their duties on board in a satisfactory manner. And this they did.

The chief steward's name was Peter Wilkin and the second steward's was Norman Cutter. They were both in their middle thirties and had no desire to leave the sea and take up jobs on land.

There was a radio officer named Walter Wright; a young man, red-haired and with a boyish face covered with freckles. He was as much captivated by the romance of the Orient as either Gregg or Loder. He had read a lot of Kipling's works in his youth, and his favourite poem was 'Mandalay', which he knew by heart and would often recite to himself when alone in the radio cabin. He would certainly not have dreamed of jumping ship. He loved the life; he loved his work, which was not onerous; and he loved going ashore in those faraway ports with their jostling crowds of dark-skinned people and the constant jabber of foreign tongues rising above the noise of traffic and patter of many feet. He enjoyed the very odours of such places, so evocative and exciting; and he deemed himself fortunate to serve on board a vessel such as the *W. H. Davies*, which carried him to these delightful parts of the world.

Even the failed attempt at piracy, which had so upset Stanley Briggs and other members of the crew, gave him quite a pleasurable thrill. It was something else to note down in his diary and to write home about. The fact that he had taken no active part in the incident made no difference; he had been there, on board that ship which had been attacked by armed criminals. And those men had been sent packing, bleeding and disarmed, by two of the ship's'company: the bosun and the cook. What a man that bosun was! In Mr Wright's eyes he had become a hero, like a character out of some tale by Joseph Conrad. Nostromo perhaps.

And again it was from this hero that Captain Gregg was to receive assistance, though of quite a different kind, in the next few days.

9
Encounter

It was the problem of finding a replacement crew now that Briggs and the others had departed that was proving difficult for Gregg to solve when Bosun Chan volunteered to help.

'You?' Gregg said. 'What can you do?'

He wondered how Chan had become aware of his difficulty. The only person on board whom he had spoken to on the subject was Frank Loder, and he was hardly likely to have confided in the bosun. So perhaps Chan had simply guessed that it might be hard to pick up the needed seamen in Hong Kong at a moment's notice.

'I know this place,' Chan said. 'I was born here. Like they say, I know my way around.'

'That may be so. But I still don't see—'

'You let me try, Captain. I get seamen. Maybe not British. You mind that?'

'Ah!' Gregg said. And he caught the drift of Chan's words. 'You're talking about Chinese seamen.'

Chan gave a faint smile. 'You not like Chinese seamen? You think they don't do good job?'

Gregg hastened to assure him that this was not so. 'You're Chinese, aren't you? You do a damn good job.'

He remembered the piracy attempt, and Chan's part in thwarting it. He was indebted to the bosun for that, no doubt about it. Yet somehow he did not altogether trust the man. Was it because he was, as he himself had pointed out, Chinese? Was it some slight racial prejudice deep down inside him that he was not fully aware of? He did not think so. So perhaps it was something else; maybe the skill Chan had exhibited in the throwing of the knife. Was that the kind of ability one would expect in a common seaman? Maybe not. And maybe Chan was a very uncommon seaman. Did it matter? He did his job; he did it well. That was all that mattered. So why not forget those niggling doubts concerning the man and accept his offer of help in picking up a new crew? It was certain that the ship would not be able to sail without one.

Chan was looking at him questioningly. 'You want me to look around? Just say the word and it's done. What have you got to lose, Captain?'

'Okay,' Gregg said. 'Take a look around.'

Like Chan said, what had he got to lose?

Later that day, in the afternoon, he went ashore; and it was in one of the bustling, crowded streets of Victoria City that there occurred an incident which, though he could not have guessed so at the time, was to have a most drastic effect on his future. And not only on his but also on that of all those others who sailed in the *W. H. Davies*.

Yet it was such a small thing really; an occurrence so common in all big towns and cities throughout the world that notice of it would hardly have been worth printing in the columns of a newspaper.

A woman had her bag snatched.

Gregg saw it happen. It was on the pavement at the foot of one of those glass and concrete cliffs that housed the many banks and other thriving businesses of Hong Kong. The woman might just have stepped out of one of them, but he could not be sure of this because he had not noticed her until he heard her cry out. His attention was drawn to her then, and he saw that she was struggling to hold on to the bag, which was a sizeable canvas holdall with a zip-fastener and a shoulder strap, while a lean, ill-dressed man was doing his utmost to take it from her. And even as Gregg watched he struck the woman a blow with his fist which staggered her and forced her to lose her grip on the shoulder strap, so that her assailant was able to gain possession of the bag and run off with it.

There were plenty of people nearby, but not one of them had gone to the aid of the woman. It was as if they regarded it as none of their business. And there was not a policeman in sight to apprehend the thief.

But Gregg had taken note of what was happening, and though he was not close enough to give any help to the woman in her struggle with the man, he was not so far away that he could not take a hand now. The thief, in making his getaway, had come in his direction, and it was an easy thing to stick out a foot and trip him up.

The result was highly satisfactory; the man lost his balance and fell flat on his face. Before he could even begin to get up Gregg planted a foot heavily on his back and held him pinned to the ground while he reached down and retrieved the stolen bag. The entire episode had taken less than a minute from start to finish.

Now he lifted his foot from the snatcher's back and gave him a kick in the ribs, which must have hurt, for it brought a cry of pain from the recipient. He got up quickly, looked at Gregg, looked at the bag, and seemed to be contemplating another attempt to snatch it. But he must have come to the conclusion that Gregg would have been a considerably tougher mark than the woman had been. So he just gave a kind of snarl, turned away and ran off, quickly disappearing from sight in the crowd. Gregg made no attempt to detain him. It was enough to have recovered the bag without getting further involved with a petty criminal who would in any case have been difficult to hold.

He turned and discovered that the woman had come up to him. At close quarters he could see that she was quite young; perhaps twenty-five or so, he would have guessed. She was not tall and was lightly built. Her hair was jet-black and short enough not to be a trouble getting into her eyes, which were of much the same colour and set rather widely apart.

Gregg liked the look of her; he liked it very much. He felt instantly drawn to her, as once years ago he had been drawn to Patricia and to no other woman since. Looking at her, he knew that here was a person from whom he could not simply walk away when he had returned her bag. There had to be more to it than that.

For a moment neither of them spoke. They looked at each other. Then he said:

'Are you all right? You're not hurt?'

'No,' she said, 'I am not hurt. Thank you so much for what you did. It was so very kind of you.'

She spoke English with a foreign accent. He could not quite place it. But he liked her voice; there was a certain huskiness in it which he found attractive.

'It was nothing. Anyone could have done it.'

'But no one else did.'

She was wearing faded jeans and a white T-shirt and a short denim jacket. Even in that gear he could see she was the right shape.

He was still holding the bag by the shoulder strap.

She said: 'Perhaps I should take it now.'

'Yes,' he said. 'Yes, of course. It's pretty heavy, isn't it?'

'Yes, it is heavy.'

She took the bag from him, but she did not say what was inside to make it so heavy. She hung it on her shoulder by the strap and it seemed to weigh her down on that side.

Gregg said: 'That was a nasty experience. He hit you. Are you quite sure you're all right?'

'Oh, yes. A little shaken perhaps – so unexpected—'

'Look,' he said. 'Why don't we go somewhere you can sit down? Have some refreshment maybe.'

'It isn't really necessary.'

'It may not be necessary, but I'd say it's a good idea.'

Certainly a good idea from his point of view. He had only to look at her to see just how good it was.

'Well—' she said. Hesitating, looking at him uncertainly, maybe debating in her mind whether it was an invitation she really ought to accept from a perfect stranger.

Gregg made her mind up for her. 'That means yes. Let's go.'

Later they were sitting at a table drinking coffee and talking and watching the world go by. Which was, Gregg reflected, a very pleasant way of passing the time. He felt pretty lucky to have been on hand when the bag-snatching took place, because otherwise he might never have met this altogether charming young woman. And that would have been a loss indeed.

He knew her name now. It was Margarita Diaz, and he gathered that she came from some state in Central America. But beyond that she had told him very little about herself.

He said: 'You are here on holiday?'

She shook her head. 'No, not holiday.'

So maybe it was business that had brought her to Hong Kong. But she did not look like a businesswoman; at least not to his eyes. Though was there any standard pattern? Might they not come in all shapes and sizes? Even this shape and this size.

He had already told her his name. Now he added the information that he was captain of a ship at present in dock waiting for engine repairs to be completed. He might have added that there was also the little matter of finding a new deck crew, but he did not. He just hoped Chan would come up with the goods, as he had promised.

She looked surprised when he told her what he was. He was not wearing anything to indicate his rank while ashore, so she could not have guessed.

'What kind of ship is it?' she asked.

'A tramp.'

She looked puzzled. 'A tramp?'

'Yes. That's a ship which goes from port to port, taking on cargo here and there, discharging it somewhere else, sticking to no fixed routes.'

'Oh,' she said, 'I see.' And it seemed to interest her more than a little, though he could not see why. 'So you are not here on holiday either.'

'Far from it.'

'And this ship, is it big?'

'Well,' he said, 'compared to an ocean liner she's pretty small, but compared to a coaster she's quite large. Four thousand tons gross, if that means anything to you.'

'It sounds a lot. And you are the captain, you say?'

'Yes. I also happen to be the owner.'

It pleased him to see that she seemed quite impressed by this revelation.

'Does that mean that you can take the ship wherever you please?'

He smiled. 'Not exactly. It depends on where the cargoes are and where they need to be taken.'

'I see. And where will you go from here?'

'It's not certain yet. But it could be Japan.'

She seemed to turn this over in her mind. And then she asked a question that surprised him.

'Do you ever go to Vladivostok?'

'We never have.'

'But there's no reason why you wouldn't?'

'No reason at all, if we had a cargo to take there.'

'Or one to bring away, I suppose?'

'Well, yes. But why do you ask?'

But she did not answer the question. Instead, she asked another one. 'What is the name of your ship?'

He told her.

She repeated the name: '*W. H. Davies*. Does that have any special meaning?'

'He was a poet. A Welshman. He wrote a book about his travels as a hobo and called it "The Autobiography of a Super Tramp". All about his adventures bumming it around the world.'

She laughed. 'Oh, I see. And your ship is a tramp. Yes, the name is most appropriate.' And then she asked: 'Tell me, does your ship have passenger accommodation?'

Again the question surprised him. 'As a matter of fact, yes. There are two cabins set aside for passengers. But nobody's ever occupied them since I've owned her. Our movements are too errratic. So they tend to get filled with all sorts of junk that has no other place to go.'

'But I suppose all that could be cleared out if someone wished to travel with you?'

'Why, yes. But so far nobody has come forward asking to be taken anywhere. And I'm not expecting anyone.' He gave her a quizzical glance. 'Unless you were thinking of making a trip. Were you?'

But again she dodged the question. She lapsed into silence and again seemed to be mulling over what he had told her.

For lack of anything more interesting to keep the conversation going, he told her about the piracy attempt in the Luzon Strait, and he could see that he had caught her attention. The knife-throwing by Bosun Chan obviously impressed her.

'That Mr Chan,' she said, 'must be quite a character. Wouldn't you say so?'

'Oh yes, he's that all right. And now he's busy finding a fresh deck crew to replace the ones that walked out on me.'

'Why did they do that?'

'Oh, they'd been discontented for some time. Reckoned we'd spent too long out east and wanted to go home. Then there was this piracy thing, which was the last straw, I suppose.'

He wondered why he was telling her all this. Not an hour ago he had never set eyes on her, and now he was confiding in her as if they had known each other all their lives. Yet somehow it seemed the thing to do. And he wanted to keep the conversation going because he hated to think of her standing up and saying that now she really had to be leaving. For that might mean he would never see her again. And he wanted to. He wanted it very much indeed.

He noticed that all the time they had been sitting there she had kept the holdall close beside her chair and had one hand clasped on the shoulder strap. It was obvious that having had one close call to losing it, she was taking no more risks. She evidently put a high value on the bag, and he wondered just what was inside it to make it feel so heavy. But he did not ask.

And then she took a sip of coffee and put the cup down and looked at him and said: 'Do you know what I would really like, Daniel?'

'You'll have to tell me,' he said. 'I'm no good at guessing.'

'I'd like to see your ship. The *W. H. Davies*. Would it be possible?'

'Why, of course it would be possible,' he said. 'I'd be delighted to take you down to the docks and show you round.' And he meant it. Offhand he could think of nothing that would have given him greater pleasure. It had been on the tip of his tongue to make just such a suggestion himself; but he had hesitated, thinking it was unlikely that she would accept the invitation, even though she had shown more than a little interest in the ship. Now it was she herself who had made the move, and he really was delighted. 'When would you like me to do it?'

'Well,' she said, 'if you've got nothing else on hand, why not now? But of course if it's not convenient—'

He quickly assured her that it was convenient. 'I'm at a loose end just now.' Even if he had had other things to do he would have put them off in favour of the chance to keep her company for a while longer.

'So as soon as you've finished your coffee we'll be on our way.'

10
Guided Tour

The MV *W. H. Davies* was lying alongside a wharf and looking, Gregg had to admit to himself, hardly the kind of vessel to make a good impression on anyone seeing her for the first time. She seemed what she was: an old workhorse of a ship that had been knocking around the trade routes of the world for too many years. The paintwork had long since lost its pristine sheen; it had become dull and chipped, while here and there streaks of rust had marked her sides and patches of red undercoat revealed where a job of repainting had been started and not yet finished.

'So this is it,' she said.

They had come to a halt a few yards from the gangplank and were gazing at this motionless ship, with her rusty anchor hauled up to the hawsepipe at the bows and the cables sprouting from her fore and aft to secure her to the bollards on the quay.

'This is it,' Gregg said. He could detect nothing in her words that might have indicated a feeling of disappointment at this first sight of the *W. H. Davies*, this somewhat less than super tramp. The comment was made without emphasis; it was noncommittal; expressing neither approval nor disapproval. 'Should we go on board?'

'Yes, of course.'

They went up the gangplank and stepped down on to the deck. A sound of hammering could be heard coming from somewhere inside the ship, probably the engine-room. There was an odour characteristic of seagoing vessels which to Gregg, accustomed as he was to it, was scarcely noticeable. There was litter everywhere: it was a kind of blight that settled on a ship in dock. It was amazing how quickly it piled up. He felt compelled to apologize for it.

'All this rubbish will go overboard as soon as we get to sea. Can't just tip it into the dock.'

'I suppose not.'

'Come,' Gregg said. 'Let me show you the works.'

She followed him as he led the way inside the midships accommodation, moving along alleyways from which doors opened into various cabins which he identified.

'The seamen, of course, have quarters aft. It's a kind of class distinction that still persists. In the old sailing ships it was the other way round: officers aft, crew in the fo'c'sle.'

He was not sure that any of this interested her. She made no comment. Moving around, they encountered few people; there was an oddly deserted feel to the ship. It was the absence of a deck crew that contributed to this. The British seamen were gone and no doubt Tommy Chan was somewhere ashore trying to collect replacements. Gregg hoped he would be successful. If he were not, there would be a problem to be solved.

They climbed to the boat-deck. He pointed out the lifeboats slung from the davits and explained how they could be launched in an emergency.

'You mean,' she said, 'that if the ship sinks you get away in these boats?'

'Yes.'

'But you don't expect that to happen, do you?'

'One never expects it, but it's as well to be prepared for anything at sea. Even in these days ships still sink. For a variety of reasons. Nothing can be guaranteed. There's no such thing as an unsinkable ship. Each year scores of them are lost. And it's not just small fry like coasters and fishing-boats. Some are monster bulk carriers, and supertankers hit the rocks and pollute the coastline for miles around. Fact is, they're just too damn big.'

She smiled faintly. 'Are you trying to frighten me?'

The question surprised him. 'Why should you be frightened? You're not thinking of sailing in one those leviathans, are you?'

'No.'

'Or one of those outsize cruise ships that carry thousands of holidaymakers out of Miami and round the Caribbean islands. You could spend a month on one of them and never even see the sea.'

'Am I to take it that you don't very much like them?'

'I hate to see what ships have come to in this day and age.'

'Perhaps,' she said, 'you should have been born in an earlier age. In the days of sail.'

Gregg laughed. 'Maybe I should.'

She asked to see the passenger accommodation. As he had said, the two cabins were full of stuff that had just been shoved in there for convenience's sake.

'So all this,' she said, 'is what you would have to clear out if you had a passenger?'

He saw that she was on that subject again; and again he asked whether she had it in her mind to take a voyage in the *W. H. Davies*.

'Would you have any objection?'

'No, none at all. But do you wish to go to Japan?'

'I have never been there,' she said. 'It might be interesting, don't you think? Where in Japan?'

'Tottori, probably.'

'Whereabouts is that?'

'On the west coast. Not many miles from Kyoto.'

She said thoughtfully: 'That would not be so very far from Vladivostok, would it?'

So now she was back on that track once more. He wondered what her interest was in that eastern outpost of Russia. He had asked her before and had got no answer. It was obvious that for some reason or other she wished to get there.

'If you call four hundred odd miles not far, I suppose it isn't. But we have no reason for going there.'

'No,' she said. 'I suppose not. At present.'

He left it at that. If she really wanted to go to Vladivostok there were surely other ways of getting there; so why should she be so keen to travel on board this old ship? He could see no reason in it.

They went up to the bridge; deserted now, with no helmsman at the wheel. She said this was all new country to her, and it seemed to interest her greatly. Gregg took her into the chartroom and showed her how one plotted a course.

'It seems very complicated,' she said. 'I'm sure I should never find my way in the sea. I'd be completely lost.'

'So would most people. It's not something you learn in a day.'

'I'm sure it's not. And you are very good at all this?'

'Good enough,' Gregg said.

They were still in the chartroom when Loder walked in. He looked surprised. As well he might.

'Hello!' he said. 'I didn't know you were back on board. And with a guest. You'd better introduce us.'

'This is Miss Diaz. We met ashore in curious circumstances, which I'm sure you'll want to hear all about,' Gregg said. He turned to the young woman. 'My chief officer and partner, Frank Loder. And my very good friend.'

He could see that Loder was favourably impressed by this unexpected visitor, especially when she smiled at him. It was a smile that would have charmed any man with warm blood in his veins. And Frank Loder had plenty of that.

'I'd really like to hear about those circumstances,' he said. 'As soon as you have the time to tell me.'

Gregg said: 'Miss Diaz is also toying with the idea of taking a trip with us.'

Loder glanced at her. 'Seriously?'

'Yes, seriously.'

'Well now,' he said. 'That would really be a turn up for the book.'

She looked puzzled. 'Turn up for the book? What book?'

'He means,' Gregg explained, 'that you would be most welcome on board.'

'Oh!' she said. 'Good!'

'And now about those curious circumstances,' Loder said.

'Later,' Gregg said. 'Right now I suggest we all go to my quarters, where we can sit down and have a talk.'

It seemed a good suggestion, and with neither Loder nor Miss Diaz making any objection, they left the bridge and went below.

*

'Now this,' Gregg said when they were in the cabin, 'is where that incident with the pirates that I told you about took place. As you can see, some of the bloodstains are still visible.'

'You told her about that?' Loder said.

'Certainly. Why not?'

'Hardly the kind of thing to attract a prospective customer.'

'I wasn't trying to attract anyone.'

'No? I thought you might have been. Anyway, tell me the other story. About how you two came to get acquainted.'

Gregg told him.

'And that's the bag that was snatched?' Loder said.

'Yes,' Miss Diaz said.

Gregg noticed that she was still keeping it close to her, as if even here she felt she could not be too careful. She obviously put a high value on it; but that was only natural. She probably had things in there which were necessities while travelling around far from home: cash, passport, maybe even jewellery, as well as changes of clothing. But, judging from the weight of it, there had to be something else besides. Still, it was none of his business what she carried around with her.

'Captain Gregg was most helpful,' she said. 'Nobody else was doing a thing, but he did.'

'It was easy,' Gregg said. 'Footballers do it all the time. It's called a foul. Sometimes a professional foul. That's when they can see no other way of stopping an opponent scoring a goal. I'd say that's what this one was. It stopped the thief scoring his goal.'

'Well, good for you,' Loder said. 'And I never even knew you could play football.'

*

The talking went on. Neither man seemed at all inclined to let their visitor go; and she for her part appeared to be in no hurry to leave. Loder went off in search of a steward to bring some refreshment in the shape of tea and biscuits; and it was getting on towards evening when Miss Diaz said she had to leave.

'You've been very kind. I've enjoyed it.'

Gregg said he would accompany her back to town. She said there was no need for him to do that, but she did not say it very emphatically, and he insisted.

'You never know who you may run into in this area. Docks are notoriously dangerous places. Your bag-snatcher is not the only shady character around, and maybe not nearly the worst.'

'Now,' she said, 'you really are trying to frighten me.'

'No. Just stating the facts.'

'Well, if you don't mind—'

'I don't mind at all,' Gregg said.

So it was settled.

11
Checking Out

The lights were coming on all over when they got off the crowded bus. Gregg had noticed that Miss Diaz kept a firm grip on the holdall during the journey and seemed to view every other passenger with a certain amount of suspicion. There could be no doubt that the earlier incident had made her nervous, and she was evidently glad to have his company. And he was glad that she was glad.

Even now he was reluctant to see her leave him. He was afraid that if he let her out of his sight he might never see her again. They had made no arrangement for any further meeting, and nothing had been settled regarding that question of her possibly occupying one of the spare cabins for a trip to Japan. Perhaps she had not after all been serious about it; but somehow he felt sure that she had been. She was not in this part of the world as an ordinary tourist, that was for sure; and there was also this odd desire to get to Vladivostok. He wondered whether the shoulder bag had something to do with it; but he could not see how it might. She was a mystery; and it was a mystery he was eager to solve.

'I don't know about you,' he said, 'but I'm hungry. How would it be if we were to go somewhere and get ourselves a meal?'

She accepted the suggestion with a lack of hesitation that he found oddly gratifying. So perhaps she was as happy in his company as he was in hers. Or maybe it was simply that she was still nervous after that earlier experience on the streets of Victoria – or even for some other reason that he had no knowledge of – and looked upon him for the present as a useful bodyguard. On the other hand, it could simply be that she was as hungry as he was and wanted to satisfy that hunger.

They found a restaurant and she kept the shoulder bag pretty close at hand all through the meal. And however nervous she might have been, it certainly had not affected her appetite.

He said: 'I hope you enjoyed your tour of the ship.'

'Oh, very much. It was most interesting. Have you always been a sailor?'

'I've had no other job. I went to training college first, and then I was apprentice on board a big merchantman.'

'And you like it?'

'I wouldn't change it for anything else. It's never boring, you see. Things are always happening.'

She smiled. 'Like being attacked by pirates?'

'That doesn't happen often. At least, not in my experience. But I believe it's on the increase. There'll always be some people who are out to get other people's possessions; if not by fair means, then by foul.'

'I suppose so,' she said. And she sounded none too happy about it; so he guessed she was thinking about her bag and whatever was in it.

He picked up the tab when they finished their meal, and she

made no argument about that. She just seemed to accept that he would pay. He did not mind. She had paid her share simply by sitting opposite to him at the table. He would have settled for that any day.

He suggested that as it was still not late they might go to some place of entertainment.

'A cinema, perhaps?'

But she was not in favour of the idea.

'I don't feel in the mood. I think I will go back to my hotel. Thank you all the same.'

'Like me to come with you?'

He thought she might say no to that too, but she did not. She seemed glad that he had made the suggestion. Maybe she still felt the need of a bodyguard in the crowded streets at that time of the evening. Or maybe she just liked his company. He would have been happy to think so.

She said the hotel was not far, and they decided to walk it, but she lost the way and it took longer than they had expected. When they reached it at last he could tell at a glance that it was not one of the top rank establishments; in fact it looked rather seedy, and he would have expected her to be staying somewhere a good deal more classy. But perhaps she was none too well-heeled and needed to watch the pennies.

She came to a stop outside the entrance and said rather hesitantly: 'I wonder if you would mind coming in with me. Just for a minute or two.'

He guessed that she was nervous of going up to her room alone, though he could not see what she was afraid of. Evidently it was something more than she had revealed; something perhaps to do with that desire to get to Vladivostok. The bag-snatching business could surely not be the sole reason for her uneasiness. But whatever it was, he was happy enough to oblige.

'Of course.'

There was a young man behind the reception desk, and Gregg thought he gave Miss Diaz a rather odd look when she asked for her key. But that might have been imagination.

The room was on the second floor. She came to the door and turned the key in the lock and walked in. And immediately she got into the room she said sharply:

'Someone has been in here.'

Gregg followed her in and took a quick look round. The room seemed tidy, nothing disordered as far as he could tell.

'What makes you think that?'

'Can't you smell it? The tobacco smoke. Someone has smoked a cigarette in here since I left it.'

Gregg detected it then. The faint lingering odour which would only have been noticeable to a non-smoker but would hang around for hours.

'A hotel worker perhaps.'

'Or an intruder.'

She went to the wardrobe, took out a suitcase, opened it and examined the contents.

'This has been searched.'

'Are you sure?'

'Yes. Someone has handled my things. I can tell. It is disgusting. And it is also frightening.'

She closed the suitcase and went to the bed. She examined it closely.

'Someone has also sat on this. Perhaps as he smoked his filthy cigarette.'

Gregg looked at it also. The coverlet was only slightly rumpled, as if whoever had sat there had taken the trouble afterwards to smooth it out with his hand.

'You see?' she said.

'Yes, you are right.'

He guessed that she had had some inkling of what she might find in the room when she asked him to accompany her. She might even have feared that the intruder, whoever he was, might be there waiting for her return. At least that fear had proved groundless.

'Was anything missing from the suitcase?'

'I don't think so.'

'So what was the thief looking for?'

She did not answer that. And it suddenly occurred to him to wonder whether this break-in could in any way be connected with the attempted bag-snatch earlier in the day. Was it the holdall and whatever it contained the object of the search? It was the only piece of her luggage she had not left in the room.

He suggested this to Miss Diaz, but got little response; just a shake of the head which might have meant anything. Then she said:

'I cannot stay here any longer. It is impossible.'

He saw that the intrusion had shaken her more than she might have admitted. She evidently feared spending another night in the room, where she would have felt most vulnerable.

'Will you go to another hotel?'

She seemed to think about this for a moment or two, a worried frown puckering her forehead. But then she gave a shake of the head.

'I'd rather not.'

'But you must go somewhere.'

'Yes,' she said, 'I must go somewhere.'

'So if a hotel is ruled out, where else is there?'

She gave him a thoughtful sort of look and said: 'Perhaps you could suggest something.'

'Me! But I hardly know my way around Hong Kong. I don't think I'm qualified to advise you on this.'

'All the same, I think you could solve the problem if you wished.'

And then he saw what she was getting at. 'Oh, I see what you mean. You're thinking of one of those spare cabins on board the *W. H. Davies*. Is that it?'

'Is there any reason why I should not take one of them and live on board while the ship is in port?'

'And when we sail?'

'We could talk about that later, couldn't we?'

Gregg smiled. 'Yes, I suppose we could.'

'So it will be all right? We go back to the ship now?'

'If that's what you want.'

He could see no objection to the idea. The fact was he liked it very much. And he had a suspicion that something like this had been in her mind even before they walked into the hotel. The discovery that the room had been entered and searched might only have served to convince her that it was time to make a move.

The suitcase was already packed, and there was no other luggage apart from the holdall. She carried this while he took the other, and they left the room and went down to the lobby. The reception clerk watched them as they walked across to the desk.

She said at once: 'Someone has been in my room while I was away. My suitcase has been searched.'

The clerk said nothing. He was a young Chinese, bony-faced, slightly-built, long-haired. There was a wary look in his eyes, as though he were prepared for trouble, could see it coming.

Miss Diaz dropped the key with its numbered tab on the desk. 'You let someone else have this key. Who?'

Still the clerk said nothing, just looked at her. Gregg thought of that adjective so commonly used for the Chinese – inscrutable. It certainly fitted this young man at this moment. He was being as inscrutable as they came.

Miss Diaz seemed to be angered by this stonewalling. She said sharply: 'Or perhaps it was you who searched my room, opened my suitcase, sat on the bed and smoked a cigarette. Was it?'

He answered then. One word. 'No.'

'But you know who it was. You do, don't you?'

But he had retreated into his shell again and was saying nothing more.

Gregg spoke to Miss Diaz. 'You won't get anything out of him. Might as well leave it.'

She hesitated, seeming reluctant to let the man off the hook. But then she evidently came to the conclusion that nothing was to be gained by harrying him further and gave a shrug of resignation.

'I suppose you're right. He is a damned villain and ought to be shot. But perhaps one day he will be. Let us hope so.' Then, turning again to the clerk: 'I am checking out right now. I could leave without paying a cent after the way I have been treated. I would be acting within my rights. But I will pay. Let me have my bill.'

The clerk produced it at once. He must have guessed that she would be checking out after going to her room, and he had it ready. She glanced at it and paid the amount without argument.

'Now let's go,' she said to Gregg. 'I have had enough of this place.'

12
Dollars

Loder was surprised to see the captain return with Miss Diaz in tow and himself carrying a suitcase. They had taken a taxi for the return journey and it was still not very late. The mate had been on deck and he met them at the gangplank.

'So what happened?'

'We'll tell you later,' Gregg said. 'Miss Diaz will be taking one of the spare cabins. Are the stewards both aboard?'

'I believe so.'

'Then get them on to clearing the cabin and putting some bedding in. The for'ard one will be best, I think.'

Loder seemed prepared to ask more questions, but Gregg cut him short. 'Explanations later. Come to my quarters as soon as you've set the wheels turning. We've got some talking to do.'

'Okay then.'

Loder went off to find the stewards while Gregg and the lady made their way to his cabin. They had not been there many minutes when the mate joined them with the report that everything was in hand to prepare things for Miss Diaz's accommodation.

'And now,' he said, 'do I get to hear why plans were changed?'

It was Gregg who told him, as briefly as possible. When he had finished Loder turned to Miss Diaz.

'So you feel yourself threatened?'

She answered candidly: 'I do.'

'But,' Gregg said, 'I still don't understand just what it is you feel threatened by. Don't you think it's time you gave us a bit more information? You're among friends here, you know.'

She seemed to give some thought to this. Then she said: 'Yes, perhaps I should. And I have to trust someone. There's so much to do, so much responsibility. And now that I am alone—'

'Alone!' Gregg said. 'You mean you had someone with you at one time?'

'Yes. My brother.'

'And where is he now?'

'He's dead. He was killed. I feel sure of it.'

'You don't know for certain?'

'No. It was in Singapore. He just disappeared. We were on this mission together. Now I have to go on alone. And it is hard.'

'What kind of mission are you talking about?' Gregg asked. He doubted whether it was a religious one. She did not look like a Jehova's Witness and it was hardly likely that the holdall was weighted down with Bibles.

'To buy arms,' Miss Diaz said.

They both stared at her.

'You're joking,' Loder said.

She gazed steadily back at him without the flicker of a smile. 'Do I look like a joker?'

He was disconcerted by this steady gaze. 'Well, no, maybe not. But then you don't look like an arms dealer either.'

'Because I am a woman? Isn't that being rather chauvinistic?

You think a woman would be incapable of handling that sort of thing?'

'Well—'

'Look,' Gregg said. 'Let's not get into an argument about something that's beside the point. Let me assure you, Margarita, that neither of us is a male chauvinist pig and we both believe in equal rights for women and all that. But now don't you think it's time you told us the whole story? It seems you could use some help, and maybe we're the ones to supply it. What do you say?'

'Perhaps you're right,' she said. 'The question is where to start.'

'Why not try the beginning? It's always a pretty good place for starting.'

'Yes, but where is the beginning? Is it years ago in a small Central American state where the democratically elected government is overthrown by a right wing army general named José Gonzalez, backed by the CIA? Is it when Gonzalez makes himself president and proceeds to line his own pockets and those of his allies at the expense of the common people?'

'Sounds like a reasonable starting point,' Gregg said. And he was thinking there was much more to this business than he had ever suspected. 'What's the name of this country?'

'Does it matter? Let us call it The Republic. It was one once, and perhaps it will be again. There is a freedom party, you see. It is fighting for the restoration of democracy. It is led by a man named Carlos Diaz. He is my father.'

'Aha! And would I be wrong in supposing that you are a member of these freedom fighters?'

'No,' she said, 'you would not be wrong.'

'And that is why you are on this mission, as you call it, to buy arms for the party?'

'Yes.'

'I'm surprised they would send someone like you on such an important errand.'

'What do you mean by somebody like me?' she demanded sharply. She seemed to take offence very easily on the subject of her capability as a woman. 'Do you think I am unable to handle such an assignment?'

Gregg hastened to placate her. 'Not at all. I just thought—'

'And anyway, as I told you, I was not alone at first.'

'Ah, of course. There was your brother. What exactly happened in Singapore?'

She frowned, as though the memory were painful to her. Then: 'I will tell you. We went there because it had been arranged that we should buy the arms from a dealer and there would be a ship we could charter to transport them. But there was no ship; it was a myth; and the dealer could not help us. However, he gave us the address of another man in Hong Kong who might be able to supply what we wanted. So we decided to come here.'

'Was that when your brother went missing?'

'Yes. The day before we were planning to leave Singapore he vanished. I stayed on for several days making inquiries but could find no trace of him.'

'You reported his disappearance to the police, I suppose?'

'Oh, yes. They were helpful, but they could find no trace of him. They did not say so directly, but they hinted that he might be dead.'

It all sounded to Gregg painfully reminiscent of his own experience in Singapore when Walter Crane, former bosun on board the *W. H. Davies*, vanished without trace. He wondered whether the body of Margarita's brother would eventually be hauled out of the waters of the harbour. But he did not mention this to her. He guessed that it might have occurred to her already.

'So that was when you decided to carry on alone?'

'What else could I do? Give up? Go home? That would have been unthinkable. I have to go on.'

Gregg admired her determination and courage. 'And have you made contact with the dealer here, in Hong Kong?'

'Yes. But he is no longer in the business. He says it is impossible under the new masters. He has decided to turn to something else. He also said that the best place to buy arms these days is Russia. He said if I went to Vladivostok I could get anything I wanted – quite cheaply. They need the money coming into the country and there's a black market for everything. So now you see why I have to get there.'

Gregg did see. But he also saw something else only too clearly. 'And when you've got there, when you've bought the arms, how do you propose to transport them to your Republic?'

'But surely,' she said, 'that is obvious. By ship.'

He raised an eyebrow. 'This ship, perhaps?'

'Of course. It is your business, isn't it? You will be paid, naturally. Have no fear of that.'

Gregg had to smile. She had it all worked out. It was all so simple, so straightforward, the way she said it. And so damned crazy.

'So you're asking us to become gunrunners. To smuggle arms to a bunch of rebels. That's illegal, you know.'

'Not at all. Those rebels as you call them are fighting for the restoration of the legitimate, freely elected government against a dictator who seized power by force of arms. How can that be illegal?'

Gregg turned to Loder. 'What do you say to all this, Frank?'

'I think the lady has a point.'

Gregg had a feeling that Loder might not have been so ready to support the lady if she had been rather less attractive. He was letting his partiality for a charming young woman cloud his judgement. But if it came to that, was not he, Gregg, in a similar case? Was he not already half inclined to do this crazy thing that she was suggesting?

'And if,' he said, 'we pick this cargo up in Vladivostok, how do we get it ashore at the other end? I don't imagine we can just sail into a port and discharge it on to a wharf for your people to come along and pick up.'

As he might have expected, she had a ready answer to that. 'You will anchor offshore at a point along the coast, and boats will come out to take off the cargo under cover of darkness. It is all arranged.'

'So I see. And you have the money to pay for all this?'

'Naturally.' She seemed to hesitate for a few moments before coming to a decision. Then: 'I had better show you. You will have to know. And I have to trust you now.'

The holdall was close to where she was sitting. She stood up and unzipped it and pulled it open. Inside were some articles of clothing, which she removed.

'There! Take a look.'

Gregg and Loder both got up quickly and took a look. And they both gasped.

'Jesus!' Loder breathed.

'Well, well, well!' Gregg said. 'What have we here!'

He had never seen so many American dollars in one batch. They were in bundles of one-hundred-dollar bills, and there were a lot of bundles. He understood now why the bag had felt so heavy.

'How much is in there?' he asked.

Miss Diaz answered coolly: 'Half a million. Rather more in fact. Six hundred thousand or so.'

And she had been carrying all this about with her, not daring to leave it in the hotel room. No wonder she had kept a watchful eye on it.

'So your lot are not short of cash?'

'You are wrong. We are very poor really.'

'Then how come you've got this little bundle to spend on arms?'

'We have a rich supporter. An American multi-millionaire, a friend of my father's. They were at college together and have kept in touch ever since.'

'And he peels off the dollar bills to keep you going?'

'You could say that.'

Loder said: 'Did you have any trouble with customs?'

She shook her head. 'Why should they make trouble? Countries like you to bring in the dollars. It helps the local economy.'

'I guess that's so.'

'But you have had trouble,' Gregg said. 'The bag-snatcher, the search of your hotel room. Above all, the disappearance of your brother. Could they all be connected?'

'I've thought about that,' she said. 'My belief is that somebody betrayed us, informed the government about this mission to buy arms. So they sent an agent to trail us and prevent our succeeding.'

'Do you suspect anyone in particular?'

'No. But there are always traitors to be found; people who can be corrupted by bribery.'

'Yes, I imagine there are. And you think this agent could be responsible for your brother's disappearance?'

'I feel sure of it. Frankly, I doubt whether I shall ever see Pedro again.' She spoke calmly, unemotionally. It was something she had come to accept. And now she herself was in danger. She had to accept that too.

'That man who snatched your bag. Do you think he is involved?'

'I suppose it is possible he was hired to do the job. It would have made it impossible for me to go on. But I think it unlikely. He was probably working for himself. A petty thief.'

'I'd say you're right. And if he'd got away with it he'd have had a surprise when he opened the bag.'

'And but for you he would have got away.'

Gregg shrugged; making light of his contribution.

Loder said: 'That man who searched your hotel room I suppose is the same one who trailed you to Singapore.'

'It seems most likely. He must have discovered where I had gone and followed me here. Perhaps he made contact with the dealer in Singapore and got the information from him.'

'Well,' Gregg said, 'however he found out, the fact remains that he is here.'

'Now look,' Loder said. 'We've all been talking as if there's only one man. Has it occurred to you that there might be two of them, or even more?'

It had occurred to Gregg, but he had not mentioned it because it might have bothered Margarita even more. But he need not have worried, for she took it in her stride.

'Yes,' she said, 'I have thought of that. It is of course a possibility. But this is all speculation and we cannot be certain.'

'Anyway,' Gregg said, 'you're not in any danger here, and you have the money. I suggest you let me lock it away for you.'

She thought about that, and it was obvious that she was reluctant to let the holdall out of her sight. But she must have seen how ridiculous this was, and she said: 'Yes, perhaps it would be best.'

She put the clothes back, so that the money was again concealed and closed the holdall with the zipper. Gregg picked it up and stowed it away in the safe.

'So now,' Miss Diaz said, 'am I to take it that you have agreed to my proposal?'

Gregg temporized. 'Let's just say that if we get this cargo for Japan we'll take you as far as that. Then we'll make a final decision whether or not to go on to Vladivostok.'

But he already knew in his heart what the final decision would be. Margarita Diaz would have her way.

She must have been sure of it too, for she did not argue the point. She just smiled and said:

'Okay. Let's leave it at that.'

13
Wharf Rats

Tommy Chan returned to the ship late next morning. He had been ashore all the previous day and all night, and Gregg had begun to worry about him. He remembered how Chan's predecessor, Walter Crane, had walked off the ship in Singapore and had never been seen again, and he could not avoid the thought that maybe he was to lose another bosun as well as a deck crew.

He was relieved, therefore, to see Chan again, and to see also that he had not come back unaccompanied: following him up the gangplank was a little band of men, all Chinese. When the bosun lined up these men on the afterdeck for inspection Gregg's immediate impression was that he had never seen a less prepossessing bunch.

Chan introduced each one by name, which Gregg immediately forgot. They were all carrying canvas bags containing their kit, which appeared to indicate that they were confident of being taken on; and each one as he was introduced gave a grin which, more often than not, revealed stained and gappy teeth. Their mien might have been described as hangdog, and all in all they were hardly the kind of men in whom Gregg would on sight have put his entire confidence.

He took Chan aside for a word in private.

'Are these all genuine seamen?'

Chan grinned. 'Oh, sure thing, Captain. Genuine article.'

'What experience have they had?'

'Fishing-boats, junks, coasters, all sorts.'

'So they know the ropes?'

'You betcha.'

'Well,' Gregg said, 'you're going to work with them. If there's any trouble you'll be the one that's to blame.'

'No trouble, Captain,' Chan said.

He appeared supremely confident, and Gregg had to take his word for it. He needed a crew, and where else could he find one?

Loder did not like the look of them, and said so. 'Wharf rats, the lot of them, if you want my opinion.'

'You're just going by the look of them,' Gregg said. But the fact was that secretly he shared Loder's opinion of the new recruits. Nevertheless, he felt obliged to defend them. 'You shouldn't judge by appearances only. They may be first class seamen. Chan vouches for them anyway, and he knows his way around.'

'Maybe he does,' Loder said. 'But I'm not sure he's altogether to be trusted. He's a shade too smart with a knife for my liking.'

'You should be glad he is. It came in very handy not long ago.'

Loder had to admit that this was so. But it did not remove his doubts regarding the replacement crew.

'They still look like a set of rogues to me.'

Rogues or not, the new men quickly settled into their quarters, and Chan had them working on jobs about the deck that needed attending to. Loder kept a sharp eye on them, but could find no fault with the manner in which they carried out their allotted tasks. Nevertheless, he was not entirely won over. He remarked to Gregg that new brooms had a way of sweeping clean.

'You're too pessimistic,' Gregg said. 'I think they'll be all right.'

'Let's hope so. Because we're stuck with them now.'

A few days later the work on the engines had been completed, the cargo had been loaded and the *W. H. Davies* had left port and was headed for Tottori on the coast of Japan.

Chan had assured Gregg that at least three of the crewmen were competent to take the wheel. And so it proved. Indeed, as the days passed, those wharf rats, as Loder had called them, turned out to be a perfectly satisfactory and willing crew under Bosun Chan's direction.

'Maybe,' Gregg remarked to Loder, 'they've been out of work and are glad to be back in a steady job. If they go on like this I see no reason why we shouldn't keep them. What do you say?'

Loder repeated his comment of new brooms sweeping clean, but he agreed that if the men continued as they had started he would have no objection to retaining them. 'At least they're better than that last lot, especially Briggs.'

Margarita Diaz had settled in very happily in the cabin which had been prepared for her, and though she suffered a slight queasiness when the ship began to roll, she recovered from it very quickly and thoroughly enjoyed this experience of sea travel, so different from anything she had known before. In her opinion it beat flying by a mile.

She was, as might have been expected, the subject of much interest on board, and a deal of idle speculation. Only Gregg and Loder were aware of the true purpose of her journey, and they had decided to keep it to themselves. Langton and Park, the second and third mates, were enchanted by her and envied the captain and mate who seemed to monopolize her company. They saw it as one of the privileges of rank, but it galled the younger men.

She took her meals with the officers and was a mystery to all but those two who refused to answer any questions concerning her. There were plenty of these fired at them until it became accepted that this was useless. Where did she spring from? And why had she chosen to take a voyage on board the *W. H. Davies,* this ancient tramp which had never under that name previously carried any passenger? They were even ignorant of her nationality, though the name, Margarita Diaz, sounded Spanish.

What everybody knew, since the information had been spread by the stewards, was that Captain Gregg had come aboard one afternoon with the young lady at his side, that the two of them had taken tea with Mr Loder in the captain's cabin, that Captain Gregg had then gone ashore with Miss Diaz, and that in the evening the two of them had returned to the ship, luggage in hand. The stewards had then been given orders to prepare a cabin for the passenger.

But this left the real mystery unsolved. Nobody knew how Captain Gregg had met her, whether by chance or design, where the lady came from, what she had been doing in Hong Kong and what had been discussed at that little tea party in the captain's cabin. Whatever the subject had been, it was surely that which had persuaded Miss Diaz to become a passenger on board the ship. It could not have been arranged before then; otherwise she would have brought her luggage the first time.

Unfortunately for the curious, what had been discussed at the party was known only to the three people who had taken part in it, and this was most frustrating for all the rest of the ship's company except perhaps for the Chinese seamen who had arrived on board only after the passenger had been installed. Mr Chan might have been interested, and he might have talked about the mysterious business to his friend, the cook; but if they had any opinions on this fascinating subject they kept them very much to themselves.

The voyage from Hong Kong to Tottori took some five days for the *W. H. Davies* to complete, and it was largely uneventful. It was in the port of Tottori, moreover, that the final decision had to be made whether or not to accede to Margarita Diaz's request and proceed thence to Vladivostok.

Gregg, Loder and Margarita held a meeting in the captain's cabin to discuss the matter, but it was really no more than a formality. All three knew that the decision to go on to the Russian port had already been taken, and it was only a matter of admitting as much.

'So,' Miss Diaz said, 'it is agreed?'

Gregg gave a wry smile. 'I suppose it is.'

It had been a decision made easier by the fact that they had been able to pick up a certain amount of cargo for shipment to Vladivostok. It was machinery; most of which was to be delivered to a Japanese timber company operating in that part of the world. Large swathes of the great pine forests of Siberia were being felled by Japanese and Korean companies who had the hard currency to pour in in exchange for the timber, and preservation had to go by the board in the face of stern necessity.

Gregg said: 'You'll need to buy some warm clothing. I don't suppose you brought any with you.'

'That's true,' she said. 'I had no idea it would be necessary. We hadn't planned to go so far north.'

Even in that part of Japan the temperature was far below what they had experienced in Hong Kong, and it would be colder still in Vladivostok as the season moved into autumn. Gregg had warned Chan of the next probable destination and had advised him to see to it that the Chinese crew members, who had come aboard with so little in the way of kit, were equipped for the cold. Chan had pointed out that the men had no money with which to buy clothing, and Gregg had agreed to give them an advance of pay to take care of this difficulty.

'But see to it that they don't just spend the cash on getting drunk when they go ashore.'

Chan grinned. 'Don't worry, Captain. I warn them – they get no warm clothes, they freeze to death. I scare hell out of those guys. They do as I tell them. You betcha.'

Gregg believed him. He seemed to rule that rough-looking crew with a rod of iron. He had the gift of authority; it came naturally to him, this ability to impose his will on those beneath him in rank.

'You ever been to Vladivostok?' Gregg asked.

'No, sir, never.'

'How do you feel about going there?'

Chan shrugged. 'Don't feel nothing. This ship go there, I go too. Sailor man, he take what come. Go here, go there – all one to him.'

So this was Chan's attitude to life. In his situation it was as good a one to have as any.

Miss Diaz said: 'How fortunate, Daniel, it was that you were there in Hong Kong to come to my rescue. I don't know what I would have done otherwise.'

'Oh,' Gregg said, 'I suppose you would just have found someone else to charm.'

She smiled. 'And I have charmed you?'

'And others,' Gregg said. 'Ask Frank. Don't pretend you didn't know.'

This time she merely smiled.

14
Secret Agent

In Hong Kong a man named Pablo Lopez was preparing to depart for fresh woods and pastures new. Mr Lopez had been making inquiries here and there, but he had completed them now and his business in this place was finished.

Pablo Lopez was unremarkable in appearance. Seeing him for the first time, one might have thought of a door-to-door salesman, a bookie's clerk, a low-grade croupier, an undertaker's assistant. He was none of these. He was in fact a secret agent, and good at his trade.

Lopez, a small, dark, sharp-nosed man, had never had any pretensions to physical attractiveness. His features were somewhat like those of a ferret, if that animal had grown a straggling black moustache and had taken to wearing sunglasses. He was slightly built and of conservative tastes in dress, and he had a habit of stroking his chin with his left hand, perhaps as an aid to the processes of thought. He did much thinking. He had been heard to remark that the brain is the most important weapon in the secret agent's armoury. And he could have been right at that; though it needed to be a peculiar type of brain.

He had arrived in Singapore hard on the heels of the brother and sister Diaz, and it had not taken him long to find them. He had seen them, though they had not seen him, and would not have known him if they had. He knew his way around in Singapore, as he did in many other cities of the world, and he knew where to find the men he needed. There were two of them, and when he had identified the mark they waited for Pedro Diaz to leave the hotel where the brother and sister were staying. He was alone. They tailed him, picked their moment to kidnap him, killed him and disposed of the body. They were professionals, skilled assassins, and Lopez paid them well. He was well supplied with cash. The government of José Gonzalez was generous in financing the work he did and knew that it was getting value for the money.

With the brother out of the way, Lopez was confident that the sister would lose heart and abandon the mission. In this he was to be disappointed. She stayed on and seemed to have every intention of going ahead with the work on her own. He thought of having her assassinated also, but hesitated to go to this extreme. And besides, there was the financial aspect of the affair. The two young people must have brought a considerable amount of money with them to finance the arms deal, and for such a transaction it would almost certainly be in cash. Pablo Lopez saw no reason why he should not get his hands on this little lot as a perquisite of the job he was doing.

He knew that Pedro Diaz had had no great amount of money on him when he was picked up by the assassins; it was unlikely that he would have had. So perhaps it was in the hotel room. It might have been banked, but he doubted this. He decided to get himself into Miss Diaz's room while she was not there and make a search.

It never came to that, however; for before he could carry out his scheme the lady left Singapore. He went to the hotel and was told that she had checked out, and they did not know where she had gone. It was none of their business.

However, it was very much Lopez's business. She could perhaps have given up after all and gone home, as he had at first suspected she would do; but now he did not believe this; did not wish to believe it. He wanted that money.

He knew the arms dealer the pair were likely to have visited in order to arrange a shipment, and he paid a visit to the man and made inquiries. He was told quite frankly that the Diazes had come but had been turned away empty-handed because the firm had abandoned that kind of business. He had advised them to go to Hong Kong, where there was an agent who would no doubt do a deal with them.

'That is where I expect they have gone if they are no longer here.'

It was obvious to Lopez that the man had not heard of the disappearance of Pedro Diaz. It had not been the kind of news item that would be likely to figure prominently in the press.

He decided to leave Singapore and go to Hong Kong, and he had not been there long before discovering where Miss Diaz was staying. The next day he kept watch on the hotel and was rewarded for his vigilance by seeing her leave in the afternoon, carrying a large shoulder bag.

He gave her time to get well away and then entered the lobby of the hotel. Judging by the poor class of the place, he felt sure it would not be difficult to persuade the young Chinese reception clerk to let him borrow the key to Miss Diaz's room in exchange for a generous bribe. In the event his judgement proved to be faultless. He took the key, went up to the second floor and let himself into the room, closing and locking the door behind him.

The search he made was rapid but thorough. He had had experience of such business. But the experience was of no avail: there was no money in the room. He had looked in the wardrobe and the drawers; he had searched a suitcase; and he had found nothing of any value. He was stymied.

He sat on the bed and gave some thought to the matter. He lit a cigarette and smoked it as an aid to his thinking; and it was then that he remembered the large shoulder bag Miss Diaz had been carrying when he had seen her leaving the hotel.

'That is it,' he murmured. 'She is keeping it with her. Clever girl!'

He had a feeling almost of admiration for her. She was smart; no doubt about that. But of course he was smarter. She would not get away with it.

He finished his cigarette, stubbed it out and put the butt back in the packet. He made sure there was no ash on the carpet and he smoothed out the coverlet on the bed where he had been sitting. Then he left the room, relocked the door on the outside and went back to the lobby, where he returned the key to the reception clerk. He then left.

It was evening when Lopez returned to the hotel. The same Chinese clerk was at the reception desk, and he inquired whether Miss Diaz had yet returned.

'No, the lady has not come in. See, there is the key to her room.'

It was irritating. Lopez had a feeling that the man was mocking him, though his face was expressionless. Perhaps the fellow guessed that his previous visit had proved fruitless. Now he would have to go away and kill more time before returning. He thought of taking a seat in the lobby and waiting there until Miss Diaz came back. His plan was a simple one. When she came in he would follow her to her room and threaten her with the pistol which he carried with him. He had no wish to kill her; but it would not be necessary. If he took the money from her she would not be able to go through with the purchase of arms anyway, and her mission would be at an end.

That idea of waiting in the lobby had its attractions. There was a seat, half screened from the reception desk, where he could sit inconspicuously and keep an eye open for anyone entering the hotel. There was no telling how long he would have to wait, but he would simply have to be patient. There was much at stake.

As matters turned out, his vigil was fairly brief. He had not been seated in his corner for more than ten minutes when Miss Diaz came into the hotel and went to the reception desk for her key. Lopez saw that she was still carrying the large shoulder bag, which was very satisfactory; but what was far less so from his point of view was the fact that she was accompanied by a man.

This was a complication that he had simply not anticipated. It had never occurred to him that she would not be alone; and if this man went up with her to her room it would completely upset his plan.

And the man did go with her.

Neither of them appeared to have noticed him; and he waited, thinking that perhaps the man would soon leave and allow him to carry out the plan after all. But when the man came down into the lobby Miss Diaz was still with him. What was more, the man was carrying her suitcase while she had the shoulder bag. There was only one conclusion that could be reached from this: late as it was, she was checking out and quitting the hotel.

Lopez almost swore out loud, but controlled the impulse. This turn of events had really scuppered his plan, and he tried to think what had made Miss Diaz come to the sudden decision to leave at that time in the evening. It made no sense to him.

Again the two did not notice him. They went straight to the reception desk, and though he could not hear all that was said, it was easy to see that Miss Diaz was pretty angry about something and that the clerk was getting the sharp edge of her tongue. He had a feeling that she was complaining that her room had been broken into and searched. This surprised him, since he had been careful to leave everything as he had found it. He had avoided dropping cigarette ash on the carpet and had even smoothed out the bed coverlet before leaving.

He could see that the clerk was not saying much. He appeared to be stonewalling and just shrugging his shoulders. And eventually Miss Diaz gave up and apparently demanded her bill. Some money changed hands, and then she left with her male companion still carrying the suitcase.

Lopez had no need to ask the clerk whether the lady had checked out; it was all too apparent. When the pair departed they had not given a glance in his direction, and as soon as they had made their exit he stood up and followed.

It was easy to tail them, since it was evident that they had no idea they were being followed and never looked back. And even if they had, it was unlikely that they would have picked him out in the crowd. He lost them only when they got into a taxi and were whisked away. But he made a note of the number of the cab, and later he was able to run the driver to earth and question him.

At first the man's memory was terribly bad, and he had no recollection of picking up a white man and woman, one carrying a suitcase and the other a large shoulder bag. He was a sly looking character and could probably tell at a glance that Lopez was in great need of the information imbedded somewhere in his brain. It took quite a generous transfer of cash to reinvigorate the memory cells and dig the information out. It then transpired that he had taken the couple to a ship in one of the docks.

'And the name of the ship?' Lopez asked.

But the memory had suffered a relapse and it took another injection of cash to revive it.

'The *W. H. Davies.*'

Lopez made him repeat the name. It seemed an odd one to him, and he thought the man might be mistaken. But the driver was adamant that this was it and that he had seen the man and woman climbing the gangplank to go on board. His English was reasonably good, and Lopez had to accept that he was telling the truth.

The news that Miss Diaz was now aboard a ship was not at all welcome to Lopez. He had to admit to himself that it was now unlikely that he would get his hands on the money that he felt sure was in the shoulder bag, and he was forced to change his plan of compaign.

The idea of arranging another assassination came into his head, but he rejected it. The proposed victim was almost certainly on board the ship for the rest of its stay in harbour, and this would make it difficult to get near her. Moreover, there would be the problem of finding a hit-man to do the job. There was a new régime in Hong Kong since he had last been there, and he was not so sure of his ground as he had once been. He had no wish to find the officers of the law taking a close interest in him, as they might if he stepped out of line.

He decided to remain inactive for the present and keep an eye on the shipping news. Thus it was that a day came when he read that the MV *W. H. Davies* had left Hong Kong and that her destination was the Japanese port of Tottori.

If Miss Diaz was still on board – and he had to assume that she was – he could see no logic in her travelling to such a place. He guessed that the *W. H. Davies* had been chosen as transport for the arms she intended buying; but Tottori was just not a likely place to find such merchandise for sale.

But of course there was no reason to suppose that she had any intention of buying anything at all in Tottori. The ship would not be staying there for ever. After discharging one cargo and maybe taking on a different one she would proceed to some other port. It was the way with vessels of that kind: here today and gone tomorrow.

Pablo Lopez obtained a map of that part of the world, and when he had examined this map he suddenly smote his forehead with the palm of his hand.

'Of course!'

On the other side of the Sea of Japan, to the north of the Korean peninsula and close to the border of China, was that eastern outpost of Mother Russia, the port of Vladivostok.

'Of course!' Lopez exclaimed again. 'Where else? It has to be!'

He immediately set about making arrangements to go there.

15

Voskov

When the MV *W. H. Davies* arrived in the port of Vladivostok Pablo Lopez was already there. He had in fact been there for quite some time and was comfortably accommodated in a room in a hotel. But of this no one on board the ship was aware. Indeed, none of them even knew there was such a person as Pablo Lopez. They would not have recognized him if they had seen him in the street; and certainly they had no inkling that this little ferret-faced man with the straggly moustache was destined to have such a startling effect on the lives of every one of them.

But Lopez was there when the *W. H. Davies* came in under the guiding hand of the Russian pilot and with the assistance of a fussing tugboat moved into her allotted berth. And Lopez was aware of this arrival. He had already made his plan of campaign and was prepared to carry it out. This time he felt sure he would not fail in his purpose.

The port of Vladivostok accommodated shipping of almost every kind. There were fishing-boats, freighters, passenger ships, ferry-boats and more besides. Its hinterland was the vast expanse of Siberia, and there the Trans-Siberian Railway found its way to the sea. Moreover, it was the home of the Russian Pacific Fleet.

Margarita Diaz was impressed. She admitted to Gregg that she had not expected anything on quite such a scale.

'One might have thought, with all the turmoil there's been in Russia since the Communists lost power and all the satellite countries broke away, that a place like this would somehow be feeling the effect. But there's no obvious sign of it. There seems to be plenty of activity in the port.'

' That's true. But I suppose a place like this will always have plenty of trade. Besides, we don't know what it was like before, so we can't make comparisons. I shouldn't be surprised if the naval base is feeling the pinch like the Russian Army.'

Further along the wharf a Japanese cargo ship was being loaded with timber. There was a chill in the air and no hint of any sun. Gregg and Miss Diaz were standing on the starboard wing of the bridge, from which vantage point they had a view of the surrounding dock area. On the foredeck some of the crew were preparing for the discharge of the cargo, and the burly figure of Bosun Chan could be seen directing operations.

'When are you proposing to go ashore?' Gregg asked.

'Tomorrow morning, I thought.'

'Do you want me to go with you?'

'If you can spare the time I should be very glad if you would.'

'I'll make the time. Frank can handle things here while I'm away.'

'Then shall we say ten o'clock?'

'Fine. There is just one thing. Your passport. Does it have a Russian visa? There could be difficulty otherwise.'

'No problem,' she said. 'The dealer in Hong Kong asked me

the same question. I hadn't at the time, so he gave me the address of a man who would, at a price, endorse my passport with the necessary. It's a forgery of course, but he assured me it would pass muster.'

Gregg wondered just how genuine the passport itself was. Travelling as she was as the emissary of a rebel movement in her country, she might have had difficulty in obtaining one by the usual means. But that was not his problem.

'And it was the man in Hong Kong who gave you the address of Vladimir Voskov?'

'Yes.'

'Well, I just hope our Mr Voskov turns up trumps, because otherwise I'm going to be short of a cargo.'

'He will. I feel sure of it.'

Gregg reflected that her feeling sure of it really guaranteed nothing. But he did not say so. Why discourage her?

It was not quite what he had expected. A prosperous dealer on Wall Street would not have been ashamed to do business in such an office. The furnishing might have come very recently from a high-class store; the equipment was state of the art. It was on the third floor, and a wide window afforded a view of a large square building which could have been a block of workers' flats erected in the Stalinist era.

Gregg and Miss Diaz had been ushered in by a smartly dressed and quite attractive young woman who was probably Voskov's private secretary. The man himself was sitting behind a massive desk with his back to the window, and he indicated chairs for them to sit on with a wave of the hand, but did not bother to get up. He, like the furnishing, would not have appeared out of place in the office of a New York tycoon. He was big and fat and balding. He was dressed in an expensive-looking blue suit and had a gold watch on his wrist. When he smiled bits of gold were revealed in his mouth. Gregg would not have been surprised if there had been diamonds in there too. Between his lips was a very large cigar, which had almost certainly been rolled in Cuba. His face, Gregg thought, was the most repulsive one he had seen in quite some time. There was something of the toad about it – in the shape, in the width of the mouth, in the hooded eyes, and especially in the texture and colour of the skin.

He spoke in a croaking voice that seemed to match his face: 'Miss Diaz. I have been expecting you.' His English was good but with a foreign accent. 'My correspondent in Hong Kong has been in touch to warn me.'

The way he said this might have implied that he had been alerted to the imminent arrival of some infectious disease. But this was probably unintentional.

'I was told,' Miss Diaz said, 'that you were a man I could do business with. You know what I am looking for?'

'Sure, sure. And you, Mr Gregg – that is your name?'

'Yes.'

'You are also in this business?'

'No,' Gregg said. 'I am captain of the ship that brought Miss Diaz to Vladivostok. I am here simply as an observer.'

'To see fair play, is it?'

'Perhaps.'

Mr Voskov laughed, holding the cigar between two pudgy fingers, toad's chin wobbling, And it suddenly occurred to Gregg that what they were dealing with here was one of the so-called Russian Mafia, the newly-rich who were making hay in the sunshine of the economic chaos that had come with the overthrow of Communism and the introduction of free enterprise.

Voskov seemed to remember his manners. He opened a box of cigars that was on the desk and offered them to Miss Diaz, who declined the offer.

'A cigarette then? There are some. American.'

'Thank you, no. I don't smoke.'

'You, Captain?'

'Me neither.'

Voskov turned again to Miss Diaz. 'Maybe you like a cup of coffee. Natasha will get you a cup. Just say the word.'

But she declined that also. 'I think we should talk business, don't you?'

'Sure. Always ready to talk business. Go ahead.'

'I believe you sell arms. That is so?'

'Sure.'

'What have you got?'

'All sorts. Pistols, kalashnikovs, heavy machine-guns, light machine-guns, field guns, anti-aircaft guns, anti-tank guns, grenades, rocket launchers, tanks. You name it, we have it.'

'Nuclear bombs?' Gregg asked.

'Them you have to order special. Take a little time.'

Voskov's chin wobbled with laughter, and the odd thing was that Gregg could not be sure whether he was fooling or not. Maybe he could really supply that kind of merchandise – at a price.

'Just the small arms,' Miss Diaz said. 'I shall wish to see what you have.'

'No trouble. You got the money?'

'Not with me. But there's plenty. American dollars. Cash.'

'I can vouch for that,' Gregg said. 'I've seen it.'

'Okay,' Voskov said. 'You want to go now?'

'Why not?'

'Right then. I order the car.'

He spoke into an intercom on the desk, talking in what Gregg took to be Russian. He switched the intercom off and said:

'Ready in five minutes. Okay?'

'Okay,' Miss Diaz said.

16
Haggling

It was a big black Mercedes-Benz, and it looked as if it might just have come straight from the factory. It was standing in front of the building, and there were two men sitting in the front. They looked like gorillas to Gregg – the human kind. Or maybe subhuman.

One of them – the one who was in the passenger seat – got out and opened the rear door. He was wearing black shoes, black trousers, a black leather jacket and a black cap. The one behind the wheel was in the same sort of garb. If their headgear had been black felt hats with wide brims, and if they had been wearing dark glasses, they would have been dead ringers for American Mafia bodyguards. Gregg had no doubt that they were both armed.

Voskov had got himself into a short sheepskin coat and an astrakhan hat. He let Miss Diaz and Gregg get into the car first and then followed them in. Despite his size, there was room for the three of them on the rear seat. The gorilla closed the door and got back in the front.

The one behind the wheel put the Mercedes into gear and they were away.

'Is it far?' Gregg asked. It was just something to say. He was not bothered how far it was.

'It depends,' Voskov said, 'on what you call far.'

Which was about as informative an answer as none at all.

'Nice car,' Gregg said.

'Nice enough, but I prefer my other one.'

'What make is that?'

'It is a Rolls-Royce,' Voskov said. And Gregg felt sure he was not kidding.

'Though of course,' he added, 'now that Volkswagen have taken over the company it has lost some of its prestige, don't you think?'

'Maybe you should try a Jaguar.'

'Oh, I have one of those as well,' Voskov said.

Which finished that particular subject. Gregg reflected that he probably also had a Swiss bank account, and maybe another one in Liechtenstein.

The journey took about twenty minutes. It was away on the outskirts of the port: a big one-story building with a corrugated asbestos roof. There was a chain link perimeter fence all round it, topped with razor wire. There was a gate, which was padlocked, and a gatekeeper's hut just inside the fence.

The driver of the car gave a toot on the horn, and a man came out of the hut. He looked like another gorilla, and there was no need to speculate on whether or not he was armed because he was wearing a leather belt with a pistol holster, and the butt of the weapon could be seen within easy reach of his hand.

He walked to the gate, peered through it at the car and the

people inside it, appeared satisfied with what he saw and unlocked the padlock with a key he had brought with him. He then swung the gate open and gave a salute as the car went past. Voskov acknowledged the salute with a lift of the hand.

'You keep the place well guarded,' Gregg remarked.

'Wouldn't you?' Voskov said.

'Yes, I suppose I would.'

The driver parked the Mercedes on the tarmac near the building and the three passengers got out. Gregg could hear dogs barking, and away to the right he could see a wire netting enclosure inside which some guard dogs were padding around and giving tongue.

'Dobermans,' Voskov said. 'They're let out at night. Nobody gets in without them knowing.'

'I can imagine,' Gregg said.

There were two big lorries standing on the tarmac, but nothing much seemed to be going on. Voskov led the way to a pair of large sliding doors which were standing open, and they went inside, the two gorillas staying with the car.

It was truly amazing, Gregg thought. The size of the building was even more impressive when you were inside. It was just one vast echoing shed, and it seemed to stretch for miles. And the stuff there was in there! You could have equipped a small army with it. Voskov had not been exaggerating when he said he could supply almost anything in the arms line. The tanks were there, the armoured cars, the field guns, the mortars, the lot.

Gregg caught sight of two or three men in overalls, but they were quite some way off and he could not see what they were doing. He guessed they were maintenance engineers or some such.

Voskov glanced at Miss Diaz, perhaps to see what her reaction to all this wealth of armament might be. But if he was looking for any expression of wonder, he was fated to be disappointed. She remained cool and not visibly impressed. She knew just what she had come for, and she had no intention of being sidetracked by any of the heavy material.

'Where are the small arms?' she asked.

Voskov gave a shrug, accepting her lack of interest in the other stuff that he had to offer.

'This way.'

It was a kind of bay, opening off the main area. There were racks where various weapons were on display: the ubiquitous kalashnikov rifle, the handguns, the machine-guns, the grenades—

'Take your pick,' Voskov said. 'You know what you want?'

'I have a list.'

She had taken a slip of paper from her pocket. Gregg thought of a housewife in a supermarket; but how many housewives ever carried such a list as this? She started reading from the list, asking the price of each article and jotting it down with a ball-point pen. There were many items, and when she had got all the prices she took out a pocket calculator and worked out some more figures. Gregg guessed she was seeing how many of each item she could buy with the cash at her disposal. At her request Voskov had quoted the prices in American dollars. It was when she had completed her calculations that the hard bargaining began.

'Your prices are of course far too high.'

'You think so?'

'Certainly. You think you can cheat me, take advantage of me because I am not a man. But it will not work.'

'You are welcome to find another seller.'

'And that is just what I will do if you do not moderate your demands. Do not take me for a fool, Mr Voskov. I can walk away and then you will get nothing.'

Gregg knew that she had no intention of walking away. She wanted the goods and she had no other arms merchant waiting in the wings to supply them. Voskov may have guessed this, but he could not be sure. And he wanted to trade; that was how he had got himself rich enough to own a Rolls-Royce, a Mercedes-Benz and a Jaguar.

The haggling went on. Gregg admired Margarita's skill and tenacity in the bargaining game. He himself had never been any good at that; it made him feel uncomfortable. So he tended to pay the asking price and get the business finished in as short a time as possible. He knew he lost money in that way, but he would never change his habits now. He was too old for that.

Miss Diaz and Voskov struck a deal at last and shook hands on it. She gave him the list of goods she required, with the quantities and prices written in. She herself kept a copy.

Voskov said: 'You drive a hard bargain. With customers like you I would soon be out of business.'

'Nonsense!' she said. 'You're getting a fair price. You know it and I know it. It was just a question of coming round to it.'

Voskov grinned. He appeared to be happy enough, so Gregg concluded that Margarita was correct in her summing up.

'When can you start sending the stuff aboard?'

'As soon as you have paid the deposit.'

'And how much will that be?'

'Fifty per cent of the total cost.'

'Fifty per cent! That is far too much.'

'It is reasonable,' Voskov said.

And there the haggling began again.

Gregg was more amused than impatient. He enjoyed seeing this spirited young woman taking on the toad-faced Russian. It was a contest between beauty and the beast, and of course there could be no doubt which side he was on. He loved her; that was the truth of it. If he had not been in love with her it was doubtful whether he would ever have agreed to this crazy proposal of hers. For whatever gloss you put on it, there could be no doubt that it was gunrunning; and that was something he would never have expected to engage in. Never in a million years.

He was not at all sure about Voskov's position. Could he have carried on this business of his without at least the tacit consent of the Russian authorities? Perhaps he had a deal with them. Perhaps a certain amount of bribery and corruption was involved. But whatever the truth of it was their business and none of his, so why bother his head about it?

She got the advance down to twenty-five per cent in the end. It was also agreed that she would bring the cash to Mr Voskov's office later in the day, and that then the goods would start being shipped as soon as arrangements had been made with the docks operators.

The total cost of the merchandise was rather more than half a million dollars, and this would leave enough money to meet any other expenses, which included the freightage.

Gregg wondered whether he could charge danger money as an extra. But it was not a serious thought; and had he not been assured that there would be no danger?

He was not sure he took that assurance too seriously either.

*

The gorillas were waiting for them in the Mercedes when they left the arms store. The one who was not driving got out again and opened the rear door for them, and they got in. The gate-keeper had seen them coming, and he had the gate open for them. He gave a salute as they went past, and again Voskov acknowledged it with a languid wave of the hand.

He offered to take them somewhere for a meal, but Miss Diaz declined the offer without even bothering to consult Gregg. She must have felt she had had enough of the arms dealer's company for the present.

They had the meal instead on board ship; and Gregg could see that Loder was dying to hear all about the meeting with Mr Voskov. But in the presence of the other officers he had to contain his impatience. These others would of course know what kind of cargo the ship would be carrying as soon as it started arriving, but none of them would be aware of its ultimate destination. How they would react when the whole truth became apparent was a question that Gregg tried to avoid asking himself. There might be a problem, but there was no point in worrying about that just yet.

Arthur Grimley, the chief engineer, was saying what a god-awful place Vladivostok was. He'd been to some dumps in his time but he reckoned this beat all.

'God-awful climate, god-awful people. Why would anyone choose to live here, I ask you?'

Harry Park, the third mate, said: 'Oh, it's not as bad as all that, Chief.' And then he reddened and seemed to be wishing he had not spoken. He seldom had much to say for himself in the presence of the senior officers, though he would talk animatedly enough to Paul Langton, the second mate, and Walter Wright, the radio officer.

Grimley turned a jaundiced eye on the young man. 'Not so bad! What do you know about it?'

'Well—' Park said, and lapsed into silence.

Langton said: 'Have you been ashore, Chief?'

Grimley shifted his attention from Park and fixed it on Langton. 'No,' he said. 'And I don't intend to.'

'So how do you know it's so god-awful?'

'I just know.'

'I've been ashore,' Langton said. 'I think the place has its points. Not that I'd want to live here, mind you.'

'Nobody in his senses would.'

'But if you had been born here—'

'Me,' Grimley said, 'I'd take damned good care not to be born here.' And with this he turned his attention to his food and said nothing more.

Later there was a meeting of three in the captain's cabin. Loder was given a brief account of the encounter with Voskov and the deal that had been made.

'So,' he said, 'you're taking the deposit to him this afternoon? Is that it?'

Miss Diaz said that this was so, and that they had better count out the money at once. 'Then we can be on our way.'

Gregg unlocked the safe and took out the holdall, and the counting began. When this was completed the deposit was stowed in the holdall and the remainder of the cash was put back in the safe and locked away.

'Right,' Gregg said. 'That's that. Now let's go.'

'And take care,' Loder warned. 'That's a lot of the old moolah to be carrying around.'

Miss Diaz gave a laugh. 'Not as much as I was carrying in Hong Kong.'

'That's true, but it's still a lot.'

'I'll be very careful,' she said.

17

Second Passenger

Lopez moved around the waterfront like a wolf seeking its prey. He found out where the *W. H. Davies* was berthed, and when the seamen went ashore he tailed them. There was a bar they patronised, and Lopez went there too. It surprised him a little to discover that the men were Chinese, but it made no difference to his plan.

It did not take him long to single out Tommy Chan as the one to deal with. Even off duty one could tell that he had an ascendancy over the rest of them, and it was no surprise to find out that he was the bosun of the ship. So it was on Chan that Lopez proceeded to cast his spell.

He took the bosun aside, bought him drinks and talked to him confidentially. He said there was a way by which Chan could make a great deal of money for himself if he was interested. And Chan listened, because when it came to a question of making money, especially a great deal of it, he was bound to be interested.

'Tell me about it,' he said.

So Lopez told him. Lopez told him the sort of money he was

talking about, and it sounded good to Chan, who had never really changed his spots since the days when he had run with the street gang in Hong Kong and had joined the Triads. He still had an eye to the main chance, hoping one day to make a real killing. And this looked like that chance, it really did. He believed what Lopez was telling him, because the secret agent had a way with him that conquered disbelief. And what was more, Chan wished to believe.

'Yes,' he said. 'Yes, I see. Tell me more.'

Lopez told him more. In that smoky, crowded bar, reeking of spirits and dirty clothing; noisy with many voices and the clinking of glasses and sudden outbursts of raucous laughter; Lopez spoke softly in Chan's ear and wove his spell with all the persuasiveness of which he was a master.

'The cargo,' Lopez said, 'will be coming on board very shortly. It will no doubt be in crates. A man like you might find the opportunity, at night maybe, to open one of the crates in the hold and take out a pistol or two with ammunition, don't you think?'

Chan indeed thought this was possible.

'The other seamen,' Lopez said. 'Do you think they would join with you when the time comes?'

Chan grinned. 'They do what I say. I got them here.' He demonstrated with the ball of his thumb pressed down on the table. He knew where he had picked them up; he knew the type of men they were. They were his.

Lopez said: 'This passenger you have on board, this Miss Diaz. She joined the ship in Hong Kong, I believe.' It was not really a question. He knew it was so.

'Yes,' Chan said.

'Do you often carry passengers?'

'In my time she's the first.'

'But there is accommodation?'

'Two cabins.'

'One of which is still unoccupied?'

'Yes.'

An idea had come into Lopez's head. It would be an addition to his original plan, but perhaps a useful one. He thought about it and saw that it had its attractions. He had not intended involving himself quite so closely; it was against his principles; he had always preferred to keep himself in the background. But perhaps in this case, the importance of which could not be overestimated, it would be an advantage to make an exception to the rule. He was not sure he could completely trust Chan to carry things out the way he wanted. So would it not be best to put himself at the man's elbow, as it were? To keep him up to the mark and see that he did not make a hash of the operation.

The more he thought about it, the more he became convinced that this was a step he ought to take.

'I think,' he said, 'I may take that spare cabin.'

Chan glanced at him in surprise. 'You!'

'Why not?'

And then Chan saw the way it was. This man did not trust him. Feared that without supervision he would not do what he was supposed to do. Well, fair enough. If the positions had been reversed would he have trusted the man? Probably not. Indeed, most certainly not.

'No reason,' Chan said. 'But I'm not sure the captain will be wanting another passenger.'

'Then I shall have to do my best to persuade him.'

And Lopez smiled, as much as to say that he did not believe this would be beyond his powers.

*

Chan had been right in thinking that Gregg might not be keen to take on another passenger. And he could not think why this fellow calling himself Pablo Lopez, who had come on board asking for an interview with him, should wish to take passage in the *W. H. Davies*.

'We're not going anywhere, you know.'

'But surely,' Lopez said, 'you must be going somewhere. You're not proposing to stay here in dock indefinitely, are you?'

'No, of course not. But what I mean is that we have no fixed itinerary. This is a tramp ship. We just go where the cargoes need to be taken.'

Lopez smiled engagingly. 'And that is just what attracts me so much. This is the kind of ship I have always wanted to travel in, wandering here and there, never in one spot for any length of time. I am a writer, and I move around, gathering material for a book I am intending to write.'

'I see.'

'So how about it?'

'I don't really think—'

'Name your price. I am willing to pay. What have you got to lose?'

Gregg gave some thought to the proposal. It would mean having to take all the junk out of the second cabin, but that was no big problem. It would also mean, of course, that Lopez would be present when the arms were transshipped to the boats off the coast of Central America. But did that matter? He could do nothing to interfere with the operation; and since the merchandise would all be crated he might not even guess what it was. So what indeed was there to lose?

Lopez had invited him to name his price, so he did just that. He named one that was so exorbitant that he felt sure it would choke the man off.

Lopez agreed to it without a moment's hesitation. Gregg immediately had second thoughts and regretted allowing himself to be persuaded into taking as passenger this man whose physical appearance did not at all favourably impress him. But he had named a price and it had been accepted. He could hardly retreat now.

So, for good or ill, he was stuck with Pablo Lopez.

Margarita Diaz was far from pleased when he told her that he had taken on another passenger.

'Have you gone crazy?'

'Not at all. What's so crazy about pulling in a bit more money? Running this ship is a business after all.'

'But he'll see the arms being taken ashore.'

'So what? The crew will see it. The other officers will see it. It'll be no secret. But once it's done, what more can anyone do about it? Even if they wished to. Which is doubtful.'

She was only partly convinced. 'Why,' she asked, 'does he want to come with us? Where does he want to go?'

'He's not bothered. He just wants to travel in a ship like this for the sake of travelling. He's writing a book.'

She made a sound that might almost have been a most unladylike snort. 'That's a likely story.'

'You don't believe it?'

'No.'

'But why not? Everybody writes books these days, mainly bad unpublishable novels. Or even bad published ones.'

'How do you know that?'

'I read it somewhere.'

'Possibly in a bad novel. Anyway, it's not true. I don't write books, you don't write books, and I very much doubt whether Mr Chan does.'

'Obviously there are exceptions,' Gregg said. But he could see that his efforts to make a joke of the matter were not having a good impression on Miss Diaz. She was frowning.

'What,' she asked, 'is the nationality of this Mr Lopez?'

'Spanish, apparently.'

'And what's he been doing in Vladivostok?'

'I don't know. Gathering material for the book, perhaps.'

He thought she might say that this too was a likely story, but she did not.

'When will he be coming aboard?'

'Within the next few days. The cabin will be ready for him then.'

'I don't like it,' Miss Diaz said. 'I don't like it at all.'

But it was a *fait accompli* and she had to accept it as such.

18

Final Payment

In due course the cargo began to come aboard. There would not be nearly enough of it to fill the holds, but fortunately the ship was already partly in ballast which had been taken on in Japan for the crossing from Tottori to Vladivostok. Chan, following out Lopez's instructions, took the opportunity in the middle of the night to go down into one of the holds and purloin two handguns and some ammunition.

He hid the weapons in his kit and bided his time. There was nothing more for him to do until the moment came. And that would not be for quite a while yet.

Pablo Lopez came aboard before the loading had been completed and took over the cabin next to Miss Diaz's. He saw the bosun going about his duties on deck but gave no indication that he had ever seen the man before, much less had a long discussion with him. Chan, for his part, scarcely glanced at the new passenger.

Lopez took his meals at the captain's table in the officers' messroom. It was there that Miss Diaz met him for the first time.

Gregg himself introduced them to each other. Lopez gave a slight inclination of the head and a smile that might have been described as wolfish. Miss Diaz acknowledged the introduction with nothing but a frigid stare, which seemed to have no effect whatever on the man.

'I am delighted to meet a fellow passenger,' he said. 'Especially one so charming. I am sure this is going to be a most pleasant voyage.'

'I cannot imagine,' she said, 'what can have given you that idea.'

This somewhat withering reply failed to disconcert Lopez. The smile remained on his face.

'Well, it remains to be seen. For myself, I intend to make the most of it. I believe we have a long voyage ahead of us. Is that not so, Captain?'

'Yes,' Gregg said. 'The Pacific is a wide ocean.'

'As Magellan discovered.'

'And met his death at the end,' Miss Diaz remarked.

'That is so. But let us hope nothing so tragic lies in wait for us. After all, we are going in the opposite direction.'

'And on a somewhat more northerly route,' Gregg said.

'I don't like the man,' Miss Diaz said. She was speaking to Gregg later. 'He makes my flesh creep.'

'I don't see why,' Gregg said. 'I don't deny that he's not the most prepossessing of characters, but not everyone can be an Adonis. It's not in our power to choose our parents, and they are bound to leave their mark on us, for good or ill.'

'I don't trust him.'

'You don't have to trust him. And if you dislike him so much, just stay out of his way.'

Which in the confined space of a small ship was more easily said than done. They were in adjoining cabins, and if at no other times of the day they were bound to meet at the meal table.

And it had to be admitted that Lopez was a good conversationalist. He had evidently been around and could tell a good story. One day he was talking about bullfighting in Madrid, a city with which he seemed to be very well acquainted. In his description of the corrida he became quite lyrical.

'It is a spectacle of immense beauty; it is a ballet with a final *pas de deux* between the matador with his cape and his sword and the bull with his horns. There is nothing in the world to match. It is magnificent.'

'It is vile,' Miss Diaz said.

Lopez raised his eyebrows in surprise, genuine or feigned. 'You think so, dear lady?'

'Of course. Any person with a grain of humanity must realize it is. Why should a dumb animal be put through such torment? All those darts planted in its shoulders to weaken it, and then the final deadly thrust with the sword. It is barbaric; a throwback to ancient Rome, the gladiatorial arena and the baying mob demanding blood.'

'Ah, but this is different.'

'Oh, certainly it is different. In the bull-ring it is only the animal that gets killed.'

'Sometimes it is the matador. He puts his life on the line. And the bulls are not ordinary ones; they are bred for this one purpose; it is in their blood.'

'And the blood flows, and the people applaud. They are themselves brutalized by the spectacle. It degrades them. Even more it degrades the country where such a so-called sport is still permitted to take place.'

Lopez smiled. 'Let me ask you something, Miss Diaz. Have you ever seen a bullfight?'

'Yes. Once.'

'And—?'

'I was sickened by it.'

'You did not appreciate the grandeur, the terrible beauty of it? You saw none of this?'

'I saw only the sheer brutality, the pandering to the basest instincts of the rabble.'

'And you, if you had your way, would abolish this splendid tradition for ever?'

'Certainly.'

Lopez shook his head in mock despair. 'I am so sorry I cannot convince you of the great damage that would be doing. It would be to throw away something that is unique and irreplaceable; a vital element in Spanish culture.'

'An element that would be better lost.'

Lopez appealed to Gregg. 'You, Captain, as an Anglo-Saxon, and therefore an independent judge in this matter, what is your opinion of bullfighting?'

But Gregg refused to be drawn into the argument. 'I have no opinion on the subject. Football is contentious enough for me.'

'Ah, football! Now that is something else again.'

'I really hate that man,' Miss Diaz said.

'Because he supports bullfighting?' Gregg asked.

'Not just because of that. Though perhaps it is a pointer to his character.'

'And that is?'

'A cruel man; perhaps evil; certainly not to be trusted; sly, underhand, double-dealing.'

Gregg thought she was in danger of becoming paranoidal where Lopez was concerned. He himself had no liking for the man, but he could see no harm in him. And the passenger was paying generously for his accommodation.

'Well,' he said, 'I'm afraid we're stuck with him now. So you'll just have to make the best of things as they are.'

She gave a sigh. 'Yes, I suppose I shall. But I have a feeling that no good will come of this.'

When the cargo had all come aboard and been safely stowed away, Gregg accompanied Miss Diaz on a final visit to Mr Voskov in order to pay the amount still owing for the arms shipment.

Voskov was in a jovial mood, as he had every reason to be, having completed a sale which no doubt gave him a handsome profit. Gregg again wondered how he got away with it. Was he working hand in glove with some department of the government in Moscow, or did he manage to get his supplies by some method of discreet bribery of high-ranking officers in the Russian army? No doubt there was so much corruption in the country that men like Voskov could get away with murder. Perhaps even literally.

'It has been a pleasure doing business with you, Miss Diaz. Any other time when you need a supply of this kind of merchandise I shall be happy to oblige.'

'I doubt,' she said, 'whether there will be another time.'

'No? Well, we shall see.'

He shook hands with both of them before they left. Gregg thought that it was like shaking hands with a bunch of uncooked pork sausages. Voskov's fingers were fat and damp and rather cold. They left him with another cigar planted in his mouth and his toadlike face creased in a smile. No doubt he had much to smile about. Yet sometime perhaps nemesis would catch up with him.

The holdall slung from Miss Diaz's shoulder weighed very little when they returned to the ship. There was a chill in the air and a few flakes of snow were drifting down from a leaden sky.

Miss Diaz shivered. 'This is a dreary place,' she said. 'I shall be happy never to see it again.'

On that point Gregg felt that he could not disagree with her.

19
Biding His Time

The MV *W. H. Davies* left the port of Vladivostok the next morning and headed eastward across the Sea of Japan. The passage of that sea was uneventful, and then she passed between the Japanese islands of Hokkaido to the north and Honshu to the south by way of the Tsugaro Strait. Coming thus into the open Pacific Ocean, the course was set for Honolulu, more than three thousand miles away.

And still nothing untoward had occurred. Miss Diaz avoided Lopez as much as possible; while he, whenever they came at all close to each other, displayed a smiling gallantry towards his neighbour in the adjoining cabin which galled her intensely. She felt sure that in some way he was mocking her, though nothing in the words he addressed to her could have been construed in that way.

'That man,' she said to Gregg, 'is a pest.'

'Does he pester you?'

'No, I can't say he does. But—'

'But he still makes your flesh creep?'

'Yes. And I continue to wonder why he decided to sail with us.'

'But he explained that. He's gathering material for a book.'

'That is what he says. But have you ever seen him writing anything? Has anyone?'

'Not that I've heard. But who's to say that he doesn't scribble away like mad in the privacy of his cabin? My dear Margarita, you worry too much. Forget Lopez. Get him out of your mind.'

'Ah!' she said. 'If only I could! But for me that is impossible. He is like a bird of ill omen.'

Lopez himself might have been cynically amused if he had been able to overhear this conversation. He could have told Miss Diaz that her misgivings regarding him were only too well founded. But she would discover this for herself when the time came; and there was no need to anticipate the revelation.

Meanwhile, the weather being fine and this greatest of all the world's oceans living up to its name, Pablo Lopez took some gentle exercise each day with a saunter round the boat-deck, from which, with elbows on the rail at one end he could look down upon the afterdeck and watch the crew carrying out the tasks allotted to them under the watchful eye of the bosun. Yet never since he had come aboard had a single word passed between him and Tommy Chan, and no one had ever seen him make any contact with this man who had once been a member of a Triad gang and had killed one of its leaders in revenge for a savage beating.

Chan, for his part, had never given any indication that he was acquainted with the passenger and expected by co-operating with him to make a considerable amount of money. Lopez had warned him that he would give the signal when the time came, and until then he and Chan were to remain as strangers to each other. Any of the Chinese seamen who might have seen the pair of them talking together ashore in Vladivostok had been warned by Chan not to mention this fact to anyone. Not that there had been any likelihood of any of them doing so, since they kept themselves very much to themselves and scarcely ever spoke to any other members of the crew.

The *W. H. Davies* made only a brief stay in Honolulu to refuel and take on fresh water and fruit and vegetables as well as other supplies. Lopez went ashore just to stretch his legs, as he put it, and to take a look at the place. It was a natural thing to do, and no one took any notice. Gregg warned him not to be late in returning to the ship, as there was a deadline for sailing. Lopez said that the captain could rely on him for that.

'I have no wish to be marooned here.'

'Are you going to take notes for your book?'

'I may do just that,' Lopez said.

But Gregg could see nothing to indicate that he was carrying a notebook. He was wearing a short-sleeved shirt and no jacket. Perhaps he was going to jot down notes in his mind.

Miss Diaz stayed on board. Lopez had in fact invited her to accompany him; an invitation which she refused with a bluntness that amounted almost to insult, but which Lopez took with equanimity and a faintly mocking smile.

She spoke of it to Gregg. 'The effrontery of the man! He did it to irritate me. He must have known I would refuse.'

Gregg smiled. 'Perhaps not. Perhaps he had hopes that you would accept. He may have fallen for you. Have you thought of that?'

'Don't be ridiculous.'

'What's so ridiculous about it? Don't you realize how attractive you are? Any man would be delighted to escort you ashore.'

'Oh,' she said, 'is that so?' And then: 'Would you?'

'Of course,' Gregg said. 'Haven't I already done so?'

'Yes. But that was on business.'

'True. But maybe next time we'll make it for pleasure. What do you say? Would you like that?'

'I'd like it very much,' she said. And she smiled too. But then the smile faded, and she added: 'But who knows when that will be? If ever.'

He saw what she meant. Because the next port of call would be no port at all; and she would go ashore while he stayed with the ship and sailed away and maybe never saw her again. He hated to think of that prospect, but he could see no alternative.

'Yes,' he said. 'Who knows?'

It was not until after the *W. H. Davies* had left Honolulu and set out on the long haul across the eastern Pacific that Gregg informed the rest of the officers that the cargo was not destined to be delivered to any port in Central America, but that the ship would anchor offshore and discharge it into boats. Arthur Grimley, the chief engineer, asked the obvious question.

'Why?'

Gregg made no bones about the situation. 'Because the arms we're carrying are not going to a legitimate government but to the opposing lot.'

'You mean rebels?'

'I suppose you could call them that.'

'What else could you call them?'

'Freedom fighters, democrats, patriots – what's in a name?'

'So,' Grimley said, 'what you're telling us is that we're doing a bit of gunrunning. Is that it?'

'In a sense, yes. Does it bother you?'

Grimley thought about this, and then said: 'Hell, no. What's the odds? Though mind you, I'd be none too happy if we had a government gunboat coming up and pumping shells into us.'

'I think that's unlikely.'

'I hope so.'

Not all the officers were assembled in the messroom for this briefing. The second mate was on watch on the bridge, and the second engineer was also on duty. They would be informed later. Gregg had decided not to tell the rest of the crew, but the news was bound to leak out and everyone would know very soon. Whether they liked it or not, there was nothing they could do about it now; and he doubted whether Chan and the Chinese seamen would care. It would all be in the day's work to them.

The two young deck officers, Paul Langton and Harry Park, found the news exciting. Langton took it in his usual nonchalant way and seemed rather amused when he and Park discussed it.

'Who'd have thought it? The Old Man a gunrunner! It must have been the sparkling eyes of the lovely Margarita that dragged him into it. Can't say I blame him. In his place I'd have done the same. Wouldn't you, Harry?'

Park flushed slightly but did not answer the question. He said: 'I suppose it is illegal?'

'You bet it's illegal. But who gives a damn about legality in that part of the world? Anyway, it's done all the time, and it's just winked at.'

'Are you sure of that?' Park sounded doubtful.

'Sure I'm sure. And even if it isn't, what the hell! You're not worried are you, Harry old son?'

'Well, no,' Park said. Though not very confidently.

'Think of it as an adventure. Part of life's rich tapestry of experience. Something to tell your children about. They'll lap it up.'

Park, who was unmarried and had no children, thought this was looking rather a long way ahead, but the mention of adventure struck a chord. Yes, he could go along with that, even if with some trepidation. And besides, how could he get out of it even if he wanted to?

A hint of what lay ahead came to the ears of Bosun Chan. He gave the faintest of smiles, for in fact it came as no surprise to him. It was John Lee, the cook, who passed the rumour on to him one morning while they were drinking their tea in the galley.

'You hear that, maybe?'

'No,' Chan said, not revealing that he had known as much ever since his heart-to-heart talk with Lopez in Vladivostok. 'You think it true?'

'Could be. We got guns in holds. Somebody buy guns, sure thing. Pay good money. Why not?'

'True. Why not?'

Chan was still waiting for Lopez to make his move. The pistols were where he had hidden them, and now that the ship was away from Honolulu and there would be no more stops before the end of the voyage he could see nothing to prevent Lopez from putting things in motion. But perhaps he was leaving it until they were closer to the coast of Central America. Well, it was up to him to make the decision, and Chan could only wait for the man to come to him. So far not a word, or even a meaningful glance, had passed between them.

So Tommy Chan waited, and the days slipped away, and the nautical miles were recorded by the patent log attached to the taffrail, its logline stretching astern to the constantly revolving propeller at the further end. The weather was good and the sun shone, so that the sea glittered under its rays, and Miss Diaz wore dark glasses and reclined in a deckchair, waiting for the day, not far off now, when her mission would be completed and the weapons in the ship's holds would be delivered into the hands of those who so urgently needed them.

And Pablo Lopez, that master secret agent, moved smilingly about the decks and spoke no word to Bosun Chan. Biding his time. Biding his time.

20
You Bet

Gregg woke to find the light on in his cabin and the cold muzzle of a self-loading pistol pressed against his forehead. And then he heard the voice of the male passenger who had stepped aboard the *W. H. Davies* in Vladivostok – Pablo Lopez.

'Good morning, Captain. A little early to wake you, I fear. You must forgive me. But it is necessary.'

The gun was taken away from the forehead, and Lopez stepped back a little from the bunk. He was no longer pointing the weapon at Gregg, but was holding it, negligently it might have seemed, at his side.

Gregg sat up in the bunk, fully awake almost immediately. He stared at Lopez.

'What the devil is this? Why the gun? Where did you get it?'

Lopez had in fact got it from Chan. He had left his own, smaller pistol in Hong Kong, believing he might have trouble bringing it into Russia. He had at last passed the word to the bosun, and Chan had given him the loaded gun and taken the other for himself. All this had happened only a few minutes earlier at about five bells in the middle watch, or two-thirty a.m. by the clock. Chan had awakened those seamen who were off watch and told them what to do. He had taken them into his confidence soon after the ship had left Honolulu and prepared them for the coup that was now taking place. He had not needed to ask them whether they were with him; they had been willing tools ever since he picked them up on the Hong Kong waterfront. He had not known then just how he would use them, or even whether he would use them at all. But he had been prepared to seize the opportunity if and when it arose. Pablo Lopez, whispering secretly in his ear, had revealed to him that the opportunity had come.

'Never mind where I got it,' Lopez said. 'That is not important. The important thing is, Captain, that you are no longer in command of this ship. As of now I have relieved you of that command and taken it for myself.'

'You! What do you know about navigating a ship?'

'Very little. But it is not necessary. I shall use the second and third officers to do that – under my instructions.'

'And do you imagine they will obey your instructions?'

Lopez smiled. 'With a gun at the head it is amazing what people can be persuaded to do.'

Gregg reflected that this was true. He doubted whether either Langton or Park would refuse to obey an order backed up by the threat of being shot. Yet how could Lopez, alone and unaided, hope to take over the ship even with a gun in his hand? It was ridiculous.

Lopez appeared to read his mind. He said: 'You must not think I am preparing to carry out this operation single-handed. I am not so foolish. I have your bosun, the excellent Mr Chan, at my side. And with him the other Chinese seamen.'

'Ah!'

'Now you begin to understand, don't you? All this was planned some time ago. In Vladivostok.'

Gregg did begin to understand. Lopez had somehow got at Chan and had corrupted him. And possibly Chan had not been difficult to corrupt. What did he himself really know about the bosun? Very little beyond the fact that he was a competent seaman.

But still the reason behind Lopez's action eluded him. What was the purpose of it?

Again Lopez answered the unasked question. 'You are wondering why I am doing this. I will tell you. You and Miss Diaz were planning to deliver this cargo of arms to a bunch of insurgents. Is that not so?'

Gregg did not answer.

'Yes,' Lopez said, 'I see it is. How you were intending to get the stuff ashore I do not know, and I do not need to know. Certainly you were not going to take this ship into the Port of Santa Marta. But that is where it will go now. And I am sure the government of Presidente Gonzalez will be highly delighted to take delivery of a consignment of arms that might otherwise have fallen into the hands of his enemies. Don't you agree?'

Gregg did not say whether he agreed or not. But he was beginning to understand much that had not been apparent to him. Such as the true character of Pablo Lopez.

'So you are an agent of that government. You have been working for them all along.'

Lopez grinned. 'Now it is all becoming clear to you. Rather too late, of course.'

'So it was you who killed Miss Diaz's brother in Singapore.'

'Not personally. But yes, it was on my instructions that he was liquidated.'

'And it was you who searched her hotel room in Hong Kong.'

Lopez admitted the fact. 'But unfortunately found nothing. If only she had left the money there! Think how much trouble it would have saved. No money, no arms purchase, no necessity to take over this ship, don't you see?'

'And of course half a million dollars for your pocket.'

'Half a million!' Lopez said. 'As much as that! And all carried around in a shoulder bag. It must have been quite heavy.'

'It was. And she nearly lost it in Hong Kong to a bag-snatcher who could not have realized the value of the contents.'

'Is that so? How interesting. And how was the man prevented from getting away with it? Did she fight him off?'

'No. I tripped the man and took the bag from him.'

'Ah! So that is how you and the lady became acquainted. It was something that puzzled me. Odd the way things turn out.'

'I should never have let you come on board,' Gregg said. 'Miss Diaz was against it. She said you were not to be trusted. And how right she was.'

Lopez was not in the least put out. 'Smart young lady, that. And gutsy. Who would have expected her to go on alone after losing her brother?' There was a note of genuine admiration in his words. 'A treat to look at, too. As I am sure you will have observed, Captain.' He gave a wink, which incensed Gregg.

'Okay, Mr Lopez. I don't suppose you came here in the middle of the night to talk about Miss Diaz. What comes next? Are you intending to stay here for the rest of the voyage, keeping an eye on me with a gun in your hand?'

'Certainly not. I thank you for reminding me that there is work to be done. When I leave this cabin I shall lock the door on the outside and take the key. You will remain here until we reach port, and I trust you will behave yourself. You may as well resign yourself to the situation, because there is nothing you can do to alter it. From this moment I shall be giving the orders.'

Gregg just looked at him.

Frank Loder, asleep in his cabin, awoke to a state of affairs that differed from the awakening of his captain only in the identity of the man who was holding a pistol to his head. In the case of Mr Loder it was Bosun Chan who was revealed in the light that he himself had switched on when entering the cabin.

Chan, having awakened the mate in this unceremonious manner, stepped back and lowered the gun, but said nothing. Loder, like Gregg, had become fully awake almost in an instant. He sat up and stared at Chan, hardly able to believe the evidence of his own eyes.

'Bosun! Have you gone mad?'

Chan shook his head and grinned.

'Then what—'

'Orders,' Chan said; as though this explained all.

'Orders! From the captain?'

Loder could not believe that this was so. Unless the madness that possessed Chan was contagious and had claimed Daniel Gregg as another victim.

'No,' Chan said, 'not the captain. Mr Lopez. He in charge now. All change, see.'

This sounded only a little less crazy than the other improbability, and Loder would have liked Chan to enlarge upon his brief statement. But the bosun was disinclined to talk as much as Lopez had done in the other cabin. He had more pressing matters to attend to.

'I go now. I lock door. You stay here. Okay?'

To Loder's way of thinking it was very far from okay. But

already the bosun was moving away. A moment later he was at the door. He took the key from the lock, transferred it to the outside, went out and shut the door behind him.

Loder heard the key grate in the lock and realized that he was a prisoner in his own quarters.

Pablo Lopez, having left Gregg locked in his cabin, made his way to the bridge, where the second mate, the chunky Paul Langton, was on duty. It was remarkable, Lopez reflected, how quiet a ship could be at that time of night. Only the steady beat of the diesels was audible, and the vessel might have been forging ahead through the still night with none but a company of dead souls on board.

He walked into the wheelhouse and saw that one of Chan's seamen was at the helm. He glanced at Lopez, and then shifted his gaze back to the binnacle, ignoring the newcomer. It was a moonlit night, and the bows of the ship could be seen through the glass of the wheelhouse. On the deck below some men were moving. They seemed to be busy on one of the hatches. Lopez, satisfied with what he saw, turned away and walked into the chart-room, where he found the second mate yawning over a chart spread out on the table.

He stared at Lopez in surprise. 'Hello,' he said. 'What brings you up here so bright and early? Couldn't you sleep?'

Then he caught sight of the gun in Lopez's hand, and his jaw dropped. 'What the devil—'

'Mr Langton,' Lopez said, 'I have to inform you this ship is no longer under the command of Captain Gregg, who for the present is confined to his quarters. In future you will take your orders from me. Is that clear?'

'No, it's not,' Langton said. 'What's going on?'

'Never mind what's going on. You will for the time being share watches with Mr Park, turn and turn about. If you do not follow my orders to the letter you will be shot in the head and your carcase will be thrown overboard to the sharks. Do I make myself clear now?'

For a moment Langton thought Lopez was joking; that this whole business was some elaborate and far-fetched prank. Then he took another look at Lopez's face and the gun in his hand and swiftly came to the conclusion that, whatever else it might be, it was no laughing matter.

'Do I?' Lopez repeated. 'Speak up.'

'Yes, Langton said, 'you do. Very clear.'

'Good. Now the first thing you will do is plot a new course. It will not be much different from the present one, merely a question of making our landfall at another point along the coast. To be precise, at Santa Marta.'

'But that—'

Lopez nodded. 'As no doubt you were about to say, that is where the legitimate government under the presidency of General Gonzalez is installed. And that is where our cargo will be discharged. The port has every facility for the operation, I can assure you.'

Langton saw that Lopez was indulging in a little banter. The second mate knew perfectly well, as everyone else on board knew, that the arms were supposed to make their way ashore by a far less normal route, and that something very dramatic must have occurred to change the plan. Obviously, this man, Lopez, was not what he had made himself out to be: a harmless traveller engaged in writing a book. He had come aboard under false pretences and was now revealing his true colours.

'So,' Lopez said. 'Shall we take it that you will do as I wish and will not attempt anything foolish? Because if you were to do that it would undoubtedly become apparent to me; and then you, my friend, might find yourself coming to a very sticky end.' And when he had said this he raised the pistol in his right hand and aimed it at a point just above Langton's nose. And Langton's mouth went dry, and some drops of sweat came out on his forehead. 'You understand?'

Paul Langton answered somewhat hoarsely: 'I understand.'

And he did. He understood very well indeed. And whatever he did, he would make damned sure he set the course that Mr Lopez desired. And he would tell Harry Park to stick to that course.

You bet he would.

21

Colt Thirty-Eight

When Walter Wright, the radio officer, walked into the room where all his equipment resided he had an unpleasant surprise; indeed, more than that – a shock. One of the Chinese seamen was already in there, and he was holding a submachine-gun which was pointing straight at Wright.

The man said something which might have been an order to stop. But Wright had already stopped; the pointed gun was enough to give him the message.

'What,' he demanded, 'are you doing in here? This is no place for you. It's not allowed.' He stuttered a little, because the weapon in the seaman's hands made him nervous. In fact it was scaring the living daylights out of him, for a closer look revealed that the man had the index finger of his right hand on the trigger, and it was all Lombard Street to a china orange that the gun was cocked. 'Now put that thing down and go away. I've got work to do, and I expect you have as well.'

It was apparent that this flow of words was having no effect whatever. The man stood his ground, and even made a threatening gesture with the gun. He uttered some more words which

Wright failed to understand; and then he advanced a couple of steps and poked him in the stomach with the muzzle of the gun.

This was too much for the radio officer, who was not a particularly courageous man. He decided that there was nothing to be gained by arguing with the man who might well be crazy and certainly had a highly lethal weapon in his grasp. So he backed away and left this evil-looking Chinese mariner in possession of what by all the rules was his, Wright's, domain. What was going on? What on earth was going on?

He had seen no one that morning, other than this man with the gun. Having got up from his bunk and had a wash, he had made his way straight to the radio room and had found it already occupied in a most irregular fashion. Now he simply had to find someone who could enlighten him regarding a situation that was certainly far from normal.

And the first person he came across was the male passenger, none other than Pablo Lopez. Normally he would have avoided Lopez, since he did not care much for the man; but in his present state of bewilderment he felt an urgent need to confide in someone. So with no introduction of any kind he blurted out:

'I have just been threatened with a gun by one of the seamen. It's an outrage. I've never known anything like it.'

It seemed to him that Lopez took this revelation very calmly. All he said was: 'Don't let it upset you, Mr Wright. The man was only carrying out his orders.'

'Orders! What orders?'

'Orders to prevent anyone from using the radio transmitter.'

Wright was taken aback. 'Has everyone gone mad? Who gave these orders?'

'I did,' Lopez said.

'You! On what authority?'

'On the authority of this,' Lopez said. And he showed the pistol he was still carrying. 'The fact is, Mr Wright, that there have been some changes in this ship during the night. For the present the captain and his chief officer are under restraint and I am in control. I will not go into details, but I must tell you that no radio signals will be transmitted until I give permission. Is that understood?'

By Mr Wright it was very far from being understood; but Lopez was already walking away and evidently intended giving no more information. Bemused and worried, Mr Wright went to find someone who could give him a fuller account of what was going on.

The news of the takeover gradually became known to the rest of the ship's company. Waking in the morning to what might have been expected to have been no more than an ordinary day of shipboard routine, they were to discover that some things were very far from ordinary. Each received the information in his own particular way, and acted accordingly.

Arthur Grimley, the chief engineer, was incensed. He had never experienced anything like it in the whole of his seagoing life. The ship had been highjacked; that was the long and the short of it. And now he had to take orders from a damned passenger, if you please. Not that it made much difference in the engine-room; routine down there was unchanged, and he gave instructions to those in his charge to carry on as if nothing had happened. There was not much else he could do, of course. But it was not right, not right at all.

Harry Park, the third mate, was made aware of the change in routine when he was awakened just before four o'clock in the morning by the passenger, Lopez, of all people, and informed that because of certain rearrangements that had been made the mate was no longer able to do his watch. As a consequence he, Mr Park, would have to relieve Mr Langton on the bridge, even though his own stint had ended only four hours earlier. Lopez explained very briefly how this alteration in routine had come about, and he showed Mr Park the pistol to add authenticity to the story.

The third mate, confused and still only half awake, was persuaded by the sight of the lethal weapon in Mr Lopez's hand that he had better do as he was told. Arrived at the bridge, he received confirmation from the second mate that Lopez was now in command of the ship, and that the captain and the mate were confined to their quarters.

'It's the devil of a business,' Langton said. 'The bastard threatened to shoot me and throw my body overboard if I didn't obey orders; his orders – you understand. I believe he meant it too. I wouldn't put it past him.'

'So what are we to do?'

'Like he said – follow his orders. No alternative. Because personally I'm none too keen on being shot in the head and being fed to the sharks. Incidentally, we're on a new course. Our destination is now Santa Marta.'

'Santa Marta! But that's the very place we were going to avoid.'

'Right in one. Seems our Mr Lopez is not what he led us to believe. Seems he's working for the guys who are top dogs in the Republic, and he's going to do his damndest to see that they get the cargo we're carrying. Somehow or other, he's managed to get Chan and the rest of the Chinese helping him. Probably bribed them. Wouldn't take much doing with that lot, if you ask me.'

'Oh dear!' Park said. 'Miss Diaz isn't going to like this one little bit.'

'That's for sure. But I'd say that in the circumstances, just like the rest of us, she'll have to lump it.'

Miss Diaz did not like it. She did not like it at all. Which was hardly surprising. She could see all the work she had done, and the loss of her brother, going for nothing. And even less than nothing; because, not only would the insurgents get no arms for their money, the government of General Gonzalez would get the same arms for free.

It was galling in the extreme. And even that was too weak a word to express her feelings., She was at the same time both despairing and infuriated. And what made it so much worse was the fact that it was Pablo Lopez himself who brought her the news of the reversal of fortune; this man whom she had distrusted from the outset, whom she had urged Daniel Gregg not to accept as a passenger, and whom she so detested. If only Dan had listened to her!

Now this same Pablo Lopez was telling her how completely he had outwitted her, and was doing it in a way that grated on her, making her feel an impulse to scratch his cheeks with her fingernails, to vent her anger in a torrent of abuse.

But with a superhuman effort of self-control she remained outwardly calm, while Lopez told her how much he admired her courage in pushing ahead with her mission even after her brother's disappearance.

'You are, if you will forgive my saying so, a woman after my own heart. Such a pity that we have to be on opposing sides. We would make such an excellent team, working together. Don't you agree?'

And Lopez smiled his wolfish smile, and for a moment she thought he was going to make a move to embrace her. They were talking in her cabin, and he might.have deemed it a suitable place for intimacy. But if the thought had come into his head, he did not translate it into action.

'I would rather be dead,' she said in a tone of disgust. 'I would feel contaminated.'

The smile vanished from Lopez's face and was replaced by an expression of deepest anger. But that passed too, and he regained his usual urbanity; though she guessed that she had touched him on the raw, and that he would not forget the insult.

'You should take care what you say. Remember that I now have command of this ship and my orders are obeyed. It would be wiser of you to have me as a friend than an enemy.'

'Are you threatening me?' she asked.

'No. Merely advising.'

'Your advice is noted. Is there anything more you have to say to me?'

'Only this. You will not be confined to your cabin. I think in your case that is unnecessary. You are free to move about the ship as you wish. But a word of warning – do not take it into your head to launch into some mad scheme to turn the tables. I am in complete control and there is nothing you can do but accept the situation as it is. Maybe they will treat you with leniency when we get to Santa Marta. Who knows?'

'I have heard,' she said, 'that General Gonzalez is not notable for being a lenient man. The people he has had tortured and executed would hardly have said he was.'

'Well,' Lopez said, 'we shall see.'

And with that he walked out of the cabin and left her to reflect on this totally unexpected change of fortune.

*

Captain Gregg, locked in his cabin, opened the safe where the remainder of Margarita Diaz's money was stowed away and took out the revolver that was also in there. It was a rather old Colt thirty-eight, and he had never fired it; had hoped never to have the need to do so. Even when it might have been needed, when the pirates boarded the ship in the Luzon Strait, it had been useless because it had not been ready at hand. Tommy Chan's knife and John Lee's cleaver had been more effective.

Now he took it out and filled the cylinder with rounds. And when he had done this he fell to thinking how he might make use of it. He thought of this and that; and every damn thing he thought of he knew would just not work. The number of times he had read in books of somebody shooting the lock off a door; but he just did not see how this was done. And besides, it would make one hell of a noise, and people would come running, and where did he go from there?

The door was not shut and locked all the time. It was opened when the steward brought him a meal, but there was always a man with a gun accompanying him. Sometimes it was Chan and sometimes Lopez. So did he try shooting it out with them? Forget it.

He was escorted by an armed guard when he went to the bathroom. Suppose he were to secrete the Colt in his clothing, take the escort by surprise and disarm him. Okay, it might be done. The odds were probably ninety-nine to one against, but it might just work. But what then? Flit from place to place, picking off the opposition one by one? That sort of thing was done in films; it made great cinema. But in real life? He had never used a revolver, for Pete's sake. It was doubtful whether he could have hit a barn door from ten yards.

The hard fact was that whatever he did in the way of heroics would almost certainly end in disaster. He was a ship's captain, not an SAS man. And besides, was there any reason why he should risk his neck for the benefit of a bunch of Central American rebels, who might, if the truth were told, be just as bad as the lot they were fighting against?

He gave some more thought to the matter. Indeed, he gave a great deal more thought to it. And then he emptied the rounds out of the cylinder of the Colt and put the gun and the ammunition back where they had come from.

22
Storm

The storm came during the night when Harry Park was doing his watch on the bridge, and he was amazed at the rapidity with which it built up. He was also, to tell the truth, more than a little scared by the ferocity of it. He wished that one of the senior officers had been with him, so that the responsibility for the ship had not been entirely his.

Not that he imagined the *W. H. Davies* to be in any danger, but even with the ballast and the cargo she was still not fully laden and was riding high in the water, and this made the effect of the mounting seas all the more severe. As she forged ahead, pitching and tossing, the propeller would now and then be lifted almost clear of the water when the stern rose. Meanwhile, the bows would be completely engulfed, and the sea would come flooding over the foredeck like water gushing over a weir.

The seaman at the wheel was stolidly doing his job and saying nothing, feet planted widely apart in order to maintain his balance. Park felt an urge to turn to him for companionship, but that was quite out of the question. If all other considerations were set aside, it had to be remembered that this man was one of the lot which had taken over the ship. He was an enemy, not a friend.

The watch seemed very long to Harry Park, and he was greatly relieved when it came to an end and the second mate arrived to take over. Langton came into the wheelhouse with a rush as the ship rolled heavily, and he had to grab a handrail to avoid falling.

'My word, Harry,' he yelled, 'this is really something, isn't it? Where'd you find this little lot?'

It was raining heavily and water was running from him in streams, but he seemed as cheerful as ever. It amazed Park; it was as if his friend were actually enjoying the experience.

Day was breaking, but the pitch-black clouds overhead disguised the fact. And still the ship was being tossed around like a piece of flotsam, as if a few thousand tons of metal and timber weighed no more than a feather.

'Saw Lopez just now,' Langton shouted. 'Looked sick as a dog. Feeling a bit under the weather, I'd say. My heart bleeds for the bugger.'

Lopez was indeed feeling very sick. As long as the ship was proceeding calmly on its way, untroubled by any disturbance of a placid ocean, he had felt perfectly all right and had eaten his meals with relish. Now, however, it was a different story, and he was forced to admit to himself that he was a poor sailor and could not take the rolling of the vessel, and above all the pitching and tossing, without the bile welling up into his throat and his head feeling as though it were about to split in halves.

He would have stayed in his bunk, for even though this refuge was constantly moving, it was better to be lying down than standing up and being thrown this way and that. But he refused to exhibit such a surrender to this weakness of the body. So he ventured out of his cabin and staggered around, clinging to anything that would save him from falling; looking like death and feeling like it also.

He found his way to the open deck, and the wind and the rain hit him with a strength he would never have imagined possible. But he clawed his way to the rail and clung to it and vomited. And it was there that Chan discovered him, and grinned at him; appearing to take delight in seeing him so badly affected by the conditions.

Chan, himself apparently quite unaffected by the erratic motion of the ship and indeed almost seeming to revel in the storm that had overtaken them, shouted to Lopez that he had better go inside. It was good advice, for Lopez was wearing no protective gear and was getting thoroughly soaked with the rain and the salt spray.

Lopez, although he resented Chan's whole attitude towards him, which was one of scarcely veiled mockery and even contempt, allowed himself to be persuaded, and also to be assisted back to his cabin by the bosun.

'Better lie down,' Chan said. 'Nothing for you to do. Leave it to us. We see to things.'

By 'us' Lopez took him to mean himself and the Chinese seamen under his command. It irked him, but he was feeling so wretched that he swallowed his pride and, again with a helping hand from the bosun, crawled on to the bunk and lay there in his wet clothes, head swimming and a filthy taste in his mouth.

'You like I get you some breakfast?' Chan inquired. 'Bacon an' egg, maybe. Plenty fat.'

There was that hint of mockery again. Chan must have known very well that a man in the grip of seasickness would be revolted by the mere mention of greasy food.

'No,' he said. 'I want nothing. Leave me.'

The ship rolled and shuddered. Chan leaned against the roll, keeping his balance with no aid from a handhold. There was a constant racket inside the vessel, as though everything were breaking loose and clattering around.

'Right then. I go. Storm soon pass. You okay then. Few days now, we make port. Get pay then. Everything fine.'

Lopez hoped so. He wondered how soon was soon. The hours could not pass too quickly for him. There were moments when he regretted the decision to take passage on this damned ship, but he knew that it had been the right course to take. He could not have relied on Chan to carry the business through on his own. A man like that would doublecross you without a second thought.

Chan left the cabin. Lopez tried to find more comfort in the bunk and failed. He had never experienced seasickness before. In the age of air travel, where was the need to go to sea? Now he knew just how distressing the complaint could be, and he knew also that there would be no respite for him until the storm had passed and the ocean become calm again. Only then would the ship cease to act like a bucking horse. Only then would the bile stop welling up from his stomach to his throat. And only then would that hammer inside his skull end its beating and grant him a moment's peace.

He tried to console himself with the reflection that everything as far as the arms shipment was concerned was going according to plan; but in his present physical state he found that the contents of his mind could do little to alleviate the suffering of his body. He simply had to endure the torment as best he could.

Meanwhile, unknown to him, a different kind of drama was taking place in the adjoining cabin. Margarita Diaz had been awakened in the night by the increasing cacophony and the erratic movement of the ship caused by the storm. Having been awakened, she found further sleep impossible to obtain, and she lay on the bunk, listening to the racket and trying to rest as comfortably as possible in the difficult circumstances.

She, unlike Pablo Lopez, was not in the least seasick; and she was excited rather than frightened by this tremendous force of nature that now had the vessel in its grip. She did not doubt for a moment that the *W. H. Davies* would weather the storm, but it was thrilling to reflect that there was nevertheless a possibility that the ship might founder. And then what? Lifeboats? She, with the others, had practised lifeboat drill and knew where to go if it came to the worst. She would be in the captain's boat, and presumably someone would let him out of his cabin in such an emergency.

Lying in the bunk and letting these thoughts pass through her mind, she allowed time to pass; but it was still fairly early when she decided to get up, put some clothes on and go out on deck to see what things looked like from there. A little daylight was already filtering through the glass of the porthole, but it was very weak.

She was wearing thin pyjamas, and she had just got her legs out from under the covers and over the side of the bunk when the door, which had not been locked, was thrust open, and one of the Chinese seamen came in and closed it behind him.

She was startled by this unceremonious invasion of her privacy, and she demanded sharply: 'What are you doing in here?'

She did not care for the look of the man. Of all that motley crew, he was one of the ugliest. She had seen him around, and once or twice he had stopped work and stared at her; but she did not know his name.

He made no answer to the question, but just stood there, leering at her.

'Go away,' she said. 'Go away at once, before I call someone.'

She might as well have saved her breath. He did not move, said nothing, remained with his back to the door. He was wearing blue trousers and a ragged shirt, open to the waist. Both were soaked with water. His feet were bare and there was a pistol stuck in his belt. The black hair on his head was beginning to recede, though she would have guessed that he was little more than thirty.

Miss Diaz got completely out of the bunk and stood up, steadying herself with one hand on the woodwork.

'Look,' she said. 'Are you going to leave, or do I have to report you to the captain?'

He gave a laugh at that. And then she remembered that Captain Gregg was imprisoned in his cabin and this man was allied to his captors.

'Damn you!' she said. 'Will you go away!'

He made a move then, but not to leave. He came towards her. He reached out a hand, and in one sharp movement grasped the upper part of her pyjama jacket and tore it open. Her small firm breasts were laid bare, and instinctively she made a move to cover them again. But the man was too quick for her; he took another grip on the jacket and ripped it off completely.

She shouted for help but knew that her cries would not be heard above the racket of the storm. The man pushed her back on to the bunk and tugged off the pyjama trousers, so that she was completely naked. She tried to fight him off, and scratched his face with her fingernails. It deterred him not at all; he was far stronger than she was, and while he held her down with one hand he fumbled at his trousers with the other.

She screamed, beating his face with her fists, pummelling him; knowing it was in vain, but doing it nevertheless.

She screamed again.

It was Chan who heard the screaming. He had just left Lopez's cabin and had taken half a dozen paces down the alleyway when he heard it. He stopped, turned, came back running. He was at the door in a moment. He thrust it open and went inside. A glance was enough to take in the situation.

'Stop that!' he snarled.

The seaman, lying half on top of Miss Diaz seemed not to hear, or chose to ignore the command. He did not stop. Miss Diaz was struggling and he was doing his utmost to hold her down with one hand while he still fumbled with the other.

Chan wasted no more words. He took one stride, whipped an arm round the man's neck and hauled him off the young woman. Then he loosed his hold and struck the man on the side of the head with his clenched fist. Helped by another roll of the ship, the blow knocked the man down, and he fell to the floor. He was attempting to get up when Chan kicked him in the groin. He let out a cry of pain and stared up at Chan with hatred.

'Dog!' Chan said. And spat on him.

He turned his head and looked at Miss Diaz, who had quickly covered her nakedness with a sheet. For a moment he had taken his eyes off the man on the floor, and this was a piece of carelessness that could have cost him his life. The man, still on the floor, hauled the pistol from his belt and fired it at Chan. The bullet went so close that it clipped the lobe of Chan's left ear and buried itself in the bulkhead behind him.

It was like a wasp sting, and it stung Chan into action. He

gave the seaman another kick, this time to the head. It was shrewdly delivered, and it knocked him senseless.

Chan picked up the pistol and stuck it in his own belt. There was blood coming from the lobe of his ear and running down his chin.

Again he looked at Miss Diaz. 'You okay?'

'Yes,' she said. She had quickly regained her composure. 'But I am glad you came when you did. Thank you.'

Chan gave a grunt which might have meant anything. He gave the unconscious man another kick, but it was merely a token one.

'Damn scum! I take him away now. No more trouble from him. Promise you.'

He stooped, took a grip on the man's ankles and dragged him out of the cabin.

Lopez, in the adjoining cabin, heard the pistol shot, audible above the other noises. Despite his seasickness, he decided that this was something he just had to investigate. So, with some little effort, he got himself off the bunk and staggered to the door. He had just reached the alleyway when Chan came out of Miss Diaz's cabin, dragging the unconscious seaman by the ankles.

'What the devil,' he demanded 'are you doing?'

Chan ignored the question. He got the seaman out of the cabin and went off with him down the alleyway. Lopez followed, asking no more questions but just waiting to see for himself what was afoot.

Chan came to the doorway at the after end of the alleyway and went through to the promenade deck, where he was met by a flurry of wind-blown rain and spray. He hauled the seaman over the sill and turned to the left, the wind in his face as he moved towards the port rails, the limp body sliding along the dripping boards.

He came to the rails and released his hold on the seaman's ankles, letting the feet drop. He bent then and got his hands under the man's armpits and lifted him into a sitting position. Another lift and he had the man on his feet and facing the rails.

Suddenly the realization of what the bosun's intention was came to Lopez. And he gave a shout:

'No!'

The word was lost in the howling of the wind and the thunder of waves crashing on the afterdeck. It had no effect whatever on the bosun. He no longer had the burden of the seaman on his arms; the man was bent over the upper rail and supported by it.

Another vicious roll of the ship sent Lopez staggering towards the place where Chan was standing. And it was at that moment that Chan stooped, took hold of the seaman's legs, heaved them up and tipped the man over the rail and into the sea.

Lopez could never afterwards tell for certain whether he really heard a last despairing cry or not. Had the sudden shock of immersion in the water roused the seaman to consciousness, to a realization of where he was and what his fate was to be? Who could tell? All that Lopez could be sure of was that it seemed to him as if a cry came out of the murk, carried on the wind. But was it a human voice that called or merely something that had its origin in his own head? The answer to that question he would never know. All he would know for certain was that Chan had killed a man for shooting off a small piece of his left ear.

Some might have said that it was an overreaction. But that was the way of Tommy Chan. It was not the first time a man had died for injuring him.

23

No Harm Done

During the storm John Lee, the cook, had much to contend with. There were iron fiddles on the stove to prevent pots and pans from sliding off as the ship rolled; but it was a problem in the galley simply to maintain one's balance without having to prepare meals as well. Twice the galley boy had fallen down with a saucepan in his hand, and of course the contents of the pan had spilled out on to the galley floor, making a slippery mess which had to be mopped up. Then the stewards would come, demanding this and that, as if everything were normal and it was as easy to provide hot meals in these conditions as in a dead calm.

So Lee was not in the best of tempers, to say the least.

But there was something else that was on his mind and making him angry and resentful: it was the fact that Tommy Chan, who was supposed to be his friend, had not told him about the impending takeover of the ship by Mr Lopez, the passenger. Yet Chan had known about it from the moment when Lopez had come aboard and even earlier; yet he had kept it to himself, had not uttered a word concerning it; so that when the coup occurred he, John Lee, was as much surprised by it as anyone else on the ship. And what made it worse in Lee's opinion was that the Chinese seamen, that load of scum from the Hong Kong waterfront, had been aware of it almost from the outset. They had known what was going to happen but he had not. It was not good enough.

So when Chan came to the galley for his customary early morning refreshment and man to man chat, Lee was sullen and not at all in a friendly mood.

'You should have told me.'

Chan excused himself. 'I had my orders. It had to be secret.'

'Orders from Mr Lopez?'

'Yes.'

'Mr Lopez is not captain.'

'He is now. He's in charge.'

John Lee did not like it. He did not approve. But what could he do? He had to go along with the new order because Mr Lopez was armed, Tommy Chan was armed, and all those damned seamen were armed too. So, even before the storm came, John Lee was a disgruntled cook. The storm merely put the finishing touch to his disgruntlement. He just hoped that Lopez and Chan and all the seamen would eventually get their comeuppance; but he did not see how that would come about. The power was in their hands.

The word that Chan had thrown one of the seamen overboard reached him via the ship's grapevine in amazingly quick time. It pleased him. It seemed to say that Chan, whom he now regarded as an enemy rather than a friend, was going crazy. He wondered whether it might not be a good thing to get rid of the bosun by putting poison in his tea, He rejected the idea only because he lacked the necessary ingredient – poison.

*

The storm did not last long. It only seemed like it to Pablo Lopez, suffering the pains of seasickness. For a while longer the sea remained troubled, but gradually it calmed and the *W. H. Davies* stopped behaving like a bucking bronco and returned to an even keel.

Lopez did not immediately shake off the effects of his indisposition, but it was not long before he felt considerably better and was able to face a plate of food without feeling nauseated. The matter of Tommy Chan's conduct in throwing the seaman overboard bothered him slightly. He had had an explanation from Chan himself, who had apparently gone to the aid of Miss Diaz when the seaman was attempting to rape her. Then the man had shot at him, nicking him in the ear; and this had put him in a rage. That was his excuse, though it was hardly the kind of defence that would stand up in a court of law. But what likelihood was there of the matter ever coming up before a judge? Very little. Certainly Lopez himself would not take any action in the matter; and whether Captain Gregg would ever be in a position to do so, or would even wish to if he was, was doubtful.

Nevertheless, Chan should not have done what he did. Moreover, he should have taken more notice of him, Lopez, who was, for the present at least, his boss. Instead of this, he had completely ignored him as he dragged the unconscious man away and threw him overboard.

This it was that troubled Lopez a little. Was Chan becoming too independent? Was he becoming just a bit too big for his boots?

Lopez dismissed the thought. It made no difference. Very soon now this business of the shipment of arms would reach its conclusion, and then Chan would be needed no more. He could go his way, whatever it might be, and Lopez would go his. It would be the end of the association. Chan would have served his purpose and could be discarded like a worn-out tool.

Miss Diaz heard of the fate of the man who had assaulted her from the second steward. It shocked her. She had no reason to feel sympathy for a man who would certainly have raped her if the bosun had not made his appearance at the critical moment. But the way in which Chan had dealt with the situation was something she would never have foreseen, and probably would never forget. It had been so brutal, so sudden, and so final.

She had not spoken to Chan since. Perhaps he was purposely avoiding her. She was thankful for that. She would not have known what to say to him.

It was the steward who also told Gregg about the incident when he brought the imprisoned captain a meal.

'That Tommy Chan,' the steward said, 'is one tough customer, and no mistake. I wouldn't want to get on the wrong side of him. Makes you wonder whether this is the first time he's killed a man. I'd be inclined to say not.'

'You could be right at that,' Gregg said.

He had taken Chan on in Hong Kong because the man happened to be available and had the right experience as a seaman, but as to his past, that was a closed book. And now of course he was in alliance with Lopez, this secret agent who had taken over the ship. Which just went to prove that you should never take a man at face value. Though in Lopez's case the face had not been much of an asset.

'Still, it was lucky for Miss Diaz he happened to be on hand at the right moment. She'd have been raped, otherwise.'

It made Gregg furious to think that she had been put at such a risk; that it should have happened on board his ship. It was just one more crime to add to Pablo Lopez's account.

While the storm raged he had still been confined to his cabin and could do nothing but wait for it to spend itself. He supposed Langton and Park were coping with matters; but they were young and inexperienced, and it galled him that he himself should not have been in control at such a time.

As long as the storm lasted he saw nothing of Lopez. He was told that the fellow was seasick, and he regretted that this malady seldom proved fatal. When the storm abated Lopez put in an appearance again, still looking a bit pale but in reasonably good health.

Gregg taxed him with the matter of the attempted rape of Miss Diaz. 'Is that the way you look after one of my passengers?'

Lopez admitted that it had been an unfortunate incident. 'But such things happen. Who is to say it would not have occurred even if you had still been in command of the ship? After all, it was you who engaged this villainous crew.'

'Under my command they kept their place. None of them would have dared to assault the lady.'

'You think not?'

'I am sure of it.'

Lopez shrugged. 'Well, let us not argue over a point that cannot be proved one way or the other. Fortunately, the bosun was at hand and no harm was done. Or at least, very little.'

'Attempted rape, followed by murder! You have curious ideas of what amounts to very little.'

'And you are too sensitive, Captain. But anyway, this is not the reason why I made this visit. I came to give you a piece of news that I am sure will interest you. I have been in touch with Santa Marta.'

'Ah!'

'Yes. Your radio officer was most co-operative.'

'With a gun at his head, no doubt.'

'It is a strong persuader. Anyway, the point is that we are now expected in port within the next day or so. I anticipate a great reception.'

'A conqueror's welcome for Señor Pablo Lopez, hero of the Republic.' Gregg spoke sarcastically, but Lopez was not in the least put out. He was obviously revelling in his triumph.

'Something like that perhaps. Without too much boasting, I think I may say I have done an excellent job for my employers.'

'And will be suitably rewarded, I have no doubt.'

'It is the normal consequence.'

'You will excuse me, I hope,' Gregg said, 'if I do not rejoice for you.'

Lopez grinned. 'I excuse you. This, I fear, is not the happiest of times for you. It is hardly likely that you will be greeted in quite the same way as I shall be. It may even be chains for you. Gunrunning is a crime; and even a failed attempt is almost as bad as a successful one. The punishment may even be capital. And what applies to you applies equally, if not more so, to the señorita; since she was the one who suborned you.'

'Damn you!' Gregg said. He could see how Lopez was enjoying himself, and he had to exert a rigid self-control to avoid springing at the man and giving him a beating with his fists.

Lopez seemed to guess what was in his mind. He said: 'Don't even think of it. I have a gun and could shoot you. You may eventually be executed – I believe they still use the garrotte – but why hasten the end? While there's life there's hope. And who knows? The people in Government House may be lenient. It is doubtful, but not impossible. For Miss Diaz, however, I fear the worst.'

24

Government House

The morning that was to be the last before the *W. H. Davies* reached the port of Santa Marta come up fine and warm. The sea shimmered in a flat calm and the ship moved placidly onward, steadily reducing the number of miles that remained between her and her destination.

As a generous concession, Lopez allowed Gregg and Loder to come out of their cabins and walk on deck. It was taking no risk; they could do nothing now to upset his plans. They were not permitted to go to the bridge, but they could walk around the boat-deck; and there they were joined by Margarita Diaz.

'I am sorry,' she said, 'that I have brought this trouble on your heads. You must be regretting that you ever set eyes on me.'

'Not I,' Gregg assured her. 'All I regret is that I allowed that swine Lopez to come aboard. You warned me not to, and I wouldn't listen. So it's my fault, really.'

'You couldn't have known.'

'I should have guessed. One look at him should have been enough.'

'Well,' Loder said, 'it's no use dwelling on that now. We have to accept that the ship's going to Santa Marta. So what are our chances when we get there? What do you think, Margarita?'

She was too honest to hold out false hopes. 'Those people are not famous for their magnanimity. The only thing that might possibly save you is your nationality, but it would be foolish to rely on that. For myself I can expect nothing good. They have harsh ways of dealing with their enemies.'

A little later Pablo Lopez approached them.

'You are enjoying the fresh air, I see.'

'We were,' Gregg said. 'But there has been a change in it now, I think. Some pollution.'

Lopez was not put out. 'You should not try to offend me. It does not help your case.'

'Does anything help it?' Loder asked.

'Not really, I think. It is probably a hopeless one.'

'What will you do with the cargo of arms?' Gregg asked.

'I imagine they will be used against the insurgents.'

'So they pay for the weapons that could kill them.'

'Yes. Ironical, isn't it?'

He stayed a little while; but nobody seemed inclined to chat with him, and he went away, moving with that kind of slinking walk that was characteristic of the man.

'I suppose,' Miss Diaz said, 'someone like that takes pleasure in ensnaring people.'

'It probably gives him a kick,' Loder said. 'As for me, I wouldn't mind giving him a kick he wouldn't find quite so enjoyable.'

The sun had gone behind a cloud. They felt a shadow on their spirits also, but this was man-produced. And the man was Pablo Lopez.

Half an hour later they caught the first faint glimpse of the coast ahead.

*

It was not the pilot boat that came out to meet them. It was a small naval gunboat. From a loudhailer came the order for the *W. H. Davies* to heave to. Shortly after that the gunboat came alongside, a Jacob's ladder was lowered and a youngish naval officer dressed in a white shirt with epaulettes, white trousers and a peaked cap climbed aboard. He was followed by another officer and four ratings, all with sidearms.

Lopez was there to greet them, and he introduced himself. 'Pablo Lopez. Special government agent.'

He made a movement to shake hands, but the officer appeared not to notice. He answered in Spanish, the language that Lopez had used.

'I am Captain Marcos. You know, of course, why I am here.'

'Certainly,' Lopez said. 'You received my signal?'

'That is so. And this is the ship that is carrying the arms?'

'Yes.'

'And on board you have a young lady named Margarita Diaz?'

'Yes.'

'My instructions are to escort you and Señorita Diaz and the captain of the ship ashore. We will then proceed to Government House. Is that understood?'

'Perfectly.'

'For the present this vessel will remain at anchor in the roads. Lieutenant Gomez and these four ratings will remain on board. Arrangements for discharging the cargo will be made later. Now, as soon as you are all ready, we will leave. You are expected at Government House, and up there they do not like to be kept waiting.'

Lopez hurried away to round up Captain Gregg and Miss Diaz. The summons did not come as any surprise to them, and they were ready to go. Ten minutes later the little party was on board the gunboat and heading for Santa Marta harbour.

A black limousine was waiting on the quayside, and they all got in. Captain Marcos gave an order to the driver, and they were away.

'I notice,' Gregg remarked, 'that there are no formalities with customs.'

Lopez gave a laugh. 'You are very important persons, and as such have certain privileges. Isn't that so, Captain Marcos?'

Although the captain had spoken only in Spanish previously, it became apparent that he understood English, for he replied in that language.

'You must not ask me any questions. My orders are simply to escort you to Government House. It is not for me to engage in any discussion with you.'

'Fair enough,' Gregg said. What of any use to them would be gained by talking to this man? It was not for him to make the decisions regarding their fate. Those who held the power would be found in the place to which they were being taken.

Miss Diaz said: 'We had better admire the scenery. There is no telling how many more times, if any, we shall have the chance to see it.'

Gregg saw Captain Marcos glance at her. He seemed about to say something, but evidently thought better of it and remained silent.

The scenery that she spoke of was really no more than the built-up area of the port, which was hardly salubrious. Soon, however, they came to the more select part, where there were some fine old houses built in the Spanish colonial style. It was apparent that, though this was a poor country, there were among its people those who were doing well for themselves.

Government House was on the eastern side. It stood on rising ground and was approached by a wide avenue that climbed gently between rows of tall trees. The building itself was imposing. It had no doubt been constructed to satisfy the vanity of a succession of presidents who had seized power by anything but the democratic process, and each of whom had added something to this structure which was alternatively known as the President's Palace.

Seeing it for the first time, Gregg was impressed by its grandeur. It was built of white stone and had a dome, which made it in some respects similar to a somewhat more famous building in Washington DC.

'Some house!'

'Yes,' Lopez said, 'it is, isn't it? You have your Buckingham Palace and we have this. You have your Queen Elizabeth and we have our Presidente Gonzalez.'

'Well, at least they have something in common,' Gregg said. 'Neither was elected.'

There was an ornate fountain in front of Government House. Water gushed from the mouths of sculpted fishes, while nymphs frolicked in the pool below. A tiled driveway skirted the fountain, and the limousine made a circuit and came to a halt at the foot of a flight of wide steps leading up to a portico of doric columns.

All except the driver got out of the car, and Captain Marcos led the way into the building. Gregg thought it was like going into a museum or a picture gallery. The entrance hall was imposing and warranted more than a fleeting glance: the statues that were probably of former presidents or military leaders who had fought for independence from Spanish rule, would have been worthy of closer examination. But they were not permitted to linger.

'Follow me,' Marcos said.

They followed him across the floor of coloured tiles and up a wide curving staircase with gilded banisters to a gallery hung with paintings which, too, they were allowed no time to examine. Marcos, like an impatient guide who had seen it all before, permitted no lagging; and finally they entered a room that was considerably longer than it was wide. It had a lofty painted ceiling and a richly carpeted floor which deadened the sound of their footfalls. There was a long, narrow table of polished wood, with chairs on each side, none of them occupied at that moment. It appeared to be either a banqueting hall or a council chamber; but no banquet was taking place and no councillors were in session.

There was in fact just one man sitting at the table, and he was at the far end. He appeared to be using it as a desk. There were some papers in front of him and he had a pen in his right hand. He was so engrossed in what he was doing that he seemed not to have noticed that four people had entered the room at the opposite end. His head was lowered over his work, so that as they silently approached it was impossible to see his face. They came to a halt at the nearest end of the table; and Marcos gave a little cough and said:

'Presidente!'

The man looked up then; and Gregg saw that he was middle-aged – possibly approaching fifty. He had a narrow, somewhat thin face, with a neatly-trimmed moustache and beard, going grey. The dark hair on his head was also going grey, though it showed no signs of receding. His nose was aquiline, his eyes bright and intelligent.

Gregg's immediate thought was: 'Can this really be the tyrant, José Gonzalez?' In his mind he had had a much different picture of the man.

And then the man at the table said: 'Margarita, my dear! It is good to see you again.'

Though he spoke in Spanish, Gregg got the drift of this greeting; and it too was surprising, and not at all what might have been expected from General Gonzalez. So could it be that this was not in fact Gonzalez?

And then he knew that it was not. Because Margarita Diaz cried: 'Padre!' And in her voice there was a mixture of astonishment and overwhelming joy.

She rushed forward just as the man himself rose from his chair and came round the end of the table to embrace her.

Captain Marcos was the only one of the group who showed no surprise. He of course had known all along what to expect. But he had said nothing; being under orders not to reveal anything. He had known that the government of General Gonzalez had been overthrown even before the signal had come through from the *W. H. Davies*, though only two days before, when no news was getting through to the ship because of the ban imposed by Lopez on the use of the radio. Thus it was he himself who had made it certain that he would walk into the trap that had been laid for him.

Yet, as was to be revealed later, it had not been an armed attack by the insurgents that had led to the overthrow of Gonzalez and his immediate henchmen; it had been a palace coup by a group of young officers of the army and navy, who had overthrown the tyrant and had invited Carlos Diaz to take over as acting president until new elections could be held to choose a democratic government.

All this they were to hear about in detail; but for the present Gregg and Lopez could only stand and watch the ecstatic reunion of father and daughter and try to figure out what this might mean to them personally. For Gregg it brought a feeling of immense relief. He had been looking at imprisonment, maybe even execution, and he had been reprieved. What could he feel but joy at such an outcome?

For Pablo Lopez, the secret agent, on the other hand, the future suddenly looked bleak. In a moment he had plunged from the peak of triumph to the depths of failure. To the former President Gonzalez, now no doubt languishing in some jail, if he had not already been executed, he had been the trusted tool who would be richly rewarded for his services; but to acting President Diaz he was a bitter enemy, and even the instigator of his son's murder. What leniency could he expect? He looked around him, seeking desperately for some way of escape, and he saw two armed men enter the room by a side door: the men he knew had come to arrest him.

25
Strange Parcel

Gregg was sitting outside a café at a table shaded from the hot sun by a coloured awning. Sitting opposite him was Margarita Diaz, looking, he thought, particularly lovely. She was also looking happy, as of course she had reason to be, since fortune had turned at the last moment decidedly in her favour.

The good citizens of Santa Marta appeared to be going about their business without a care in the world; and he could only suppose they were content with the change of government. Others, who perhaps had no business to go about, or were simply neglecting it, were idling away their time as he and Miss Diaz were; while yet others, unshaven and raggedly-dressed, were trying to keep the wolf from the door by begging.

Street photographers were plying their trade; and one of these came up and took a snaphot of Gregg and his companion. He grinned at them and left his card.

'Will you buy the photo?' Miss Diaz asked.

'You bet I will. I'll keep it as a souvenir.'

She lifted an eyebrow. 'So that you can remember me when you're gone?'

'I wouldn't need a picture to remind me of that.'

'I wonder,' she said. And she looked thoughtful, frowning slightly, as though the prospect of his going away were not a pleasant one. 'Yes, I do really wonder.'

He did not ask her what she wondered. He said: 'It's odd the way things work out. All that trouble you had getting to Vladivostok to buy arms. All the trouble with Lopez and Chan and the other Chinese seamen. And in the end it turned out to have been quite unnecessary.'

'And the trouble it caused you too,' she said. 'I'm sorry you had to be involved.'

'There's no need to be. If it had not been for that I'd never have met you.'

'And you are glad you did?'

'Very glad.'

'Then I am too,' she said.

Then they were both silent for a while; just looking at each other and maybe thinking similar thoughts but not putting them into words.

It was Gregg who broke the silence. 'Odd that business concerning Chan, don't you think?'

'Yes,' she said. 'Very odd.'

The facts as known were that Tommy Chan had gone missing during the night when the *W. H. Davies* was lying at anchor in the roads. No one knew where he had gone, and questioning the Chinese members of the crew yielded no result. They all said they knew nothing; which might have been the truth and might not.

Nothing was seen or heard of him until the cargo was being discharged in the docks. Then some of the dockers came across a strange parcel in number three hold. It was a very large parcel, about six feet long, the wrapping being sailcloth tied up with cord. It was giving off a curious odour, not at all pleasant. When it was untied to see what was inside, the dead body of Bosun Chan was discovered.

The cause of death was not difficult to determine. His throat had been slit, probably with a knife, and there was dried blood all over his chest, already turning dark in colour.

But who had done the deed? Suspicion immediately fell on the Chinese seamen. Chan had thrown one of their comrades overboard, and they were a closely bound little community. The killing of the bosun had almost certainly been an act of revenge.

These seamen would certainly have been questioned again if they had still been available; but they were not. Mysteriously, they had all disappeared. No one had seen them go. But a boat had been stolen from the harbour in the night without being noticed, and it was assumed that the seamen had taken it. Two days later it was discovered abandoned some miles to the north in a small creek.

Of the Chinese crewmen there was no sign. It was as if they had vanished into thin air.

'When will you be leaving?' Miss Diaz asked.

'I'm not sure,' Gregg said. 'I have to collect a bosun and a crew. They may have to be flown in, and it could take some time.'

Fortunately, he was not pushed for cash. He had been paid generously for the use of his ship, and he was in no hurry to depart. Loder and the rest of the ship's company were also happy enough to spend some time relaxing in Santa Marta. There were worse places in which to pass a few weeks after a long sea voyage.

'And when you do leave, where will you go?'

'Wherever I think there's a cargo to be picked up. Maybe I'll take the ship back to England. It's a long time since we've been there.'

'I've never been to England,' she said. Musingly.

'There's passenger accommodation,' Gregg said. 'It might be worth thinking about.'

She smiled. 'Yes, it might, mightn't it?'